VIETNAM VENGEANCE

ONE Divided by TWO

KEITH KLUIS

Creative Force Press

Creative Force Press

Vietnam Vengeance
© 2015 by Keith Kluis
www.keithkluis.com

This title is also available as an eBook. Visit
www.CreativeForcePress.com/titles for more information.

Published by Creative Force Press
4704 Pacific Ave, Suite C, Lacey, WA 98503
www.CreativeForcePress.com

ISBN: 978-1-939989-18-5

Printed in the United States of America

This book is dedicated to the men and women of our armed services: all who sacrificed some and many who sacrificed all.

To their family and friends: many who lived each day praying their loved one would make it home, and then lived (or tried to) with the fallout as their soldier came home, trying to adjust to life after war. Many times, this adjustment is much harder and longer lasting than most people comprehend.

Please take the time to read and care about the struggle and difficulty our returning soldiers experience. Nearly every day there are stories to be found in any major news source.

He who thinks all wars
are bad has a blind eye

He who thinks all wars
are good has a blind soul

-K Robert Kloos

1

JANUARY 1973
THE START

Why is it, thought Paul, *that I hate waiting so much?* The atmosphere in this businessmen's lounge was certainly comfortable. Stuffed leather arm chairs, short-skirted waitresses dressed in low-cut outfits, low-level lighting, and people mechanically moving around him but noticing no one. He had been in many of these before joining the Army. He liked it then, but it felt different today, just two weeks after returning from Vietnam. *A lot of things feel different now*, he thought. Glancing at his watch he noticed it was now 7:15. *Where is Chris?*

He fidgeted in his chair, motioning to a waitress. "Bring me a vodka seven," he heard himself say, realizing that even the thought of Chris Stone caused his mind to drift, sliding into another day, another time.

"God, how I try to forget," he mumbled.

That scene had replayed hundreds of times in his mind. The three of them walking down a bombed-out street in Nam: Jess Whitfield, Bill Lux and himself. Navigating the cluttered city streets, they were going to meet Chris for an evening of R&R. The horror of the next 60 seconds always came to him in grotesque, slow motion. There was Chris, rounding the corner and coming toward the three of them. Paul quickened his pace, moving ahead of Jess and Bill to greet Chris first. A quick movement from behind the three men caught his eye. *Oh God, no...* Looking down, he spotted a grenade lobbed by a Viet Cong rolling to a stop between Jess and Bill. He dove into a doorway, but they had no place to escape. A loud explosion. Blood and pieces of bodies went flying. The smell of burnt flesh and gunpowder.

What could he do? He stood, numbed, for an eternity of seconds. The VC perpetrator had disappeared, and so had the young lives of his friends.

The MP's came. He answered their questions. That part was a blur. As far as the authorities were concerned, they might have been talking about stolen typewriters. They were cold, insensitive, like they had no feelings. *Where were the big boys that decided we should be in this war? Back in Washington, that's where. Nice and safe, the dirty b....'s.*

"You want this on a tab?" a sultry voice had pierced his thoughts and brought him back to his chair in the lounge.

"Uh, no." He reached for his wallet. "Keep the change," he replied. Sweat. He was sweating. A cold sweat, no less. *Why the hell can't I forget? Why the hell should I? Somebody is going to pay.*

Looking around, Paul spotted Chris. He was talking to the hostess while glancing around. Their eyes met. Chris smiled and waved off the hostess as he walked briskly to Paul's table.

Except for height and a little more bulk, Chris was a lot like Paul. They could easily be mistaken for brothers. Chris was a solidly built, 5'-10" man with wavy black hair – a nice compliment to his permanent tan. He walked easily with the grace of a gifted athlete, which he was. His rugged features stereotyped him as an outdoor worker. In fact, he had spent many hours working for his father's construction company. It was hard physical work, but Chris enjoyed working with his hands. Building and construction gave him satisfaction and a sense of importance, and he was built for it.

Paul was one year older than Chris, although at 24 years old, it didn't show. What *did* show was Chris' uneasiness in this upscale lounge. He was more at home in a dank corner bar than here. Even though he had changed into a turtleneck and stylish brown slacks, which would be a standout in his neighborhood, he now felt out of place among the gray-vested suits all around him. Paul stood up to greet Chris as he approached.

"Glad to see you again, Chris, hope you didn't have too much trouble finding the place."

"No trouble," replied Chris, "just ran into a little traffic delay—accident I think. No problem. Yeah, nice to see you again too, Paul. It's been, what, two weeks since we got off the plane from Nam?"

"Two weeks ago today," said Paul. "Seems like years." Paul was watching Chris' eyes to see what reaction might be visible. None. *Wonder if he's got it sorted out for himself*, thought Paul. *We were both pretty vocal about the establishment after what happened to Jess and Bill, and the thousands of others needlessly killed.* They had talked while on the way home about doing something to even the score. Paul was wondering how Chris felt about it after two weeks back home. *Might as well find out if I've got a partner or if I'm the Lone Ranger in this plan*, Paul had thought before their phone call yesterday.

"Chris," Paul started, "let's get right to the point. We want to do something to even the score for Jess and Bill and all the Jess' and Bill's in Nam. I've thought about it for two weeks now, and thought I might mellow, but my resolve seems to be deepening. The more I think about what is really happening, the madder I get."

While Paul talked, Chris was observing. Paul was also tan with wavy black hair, and though four inches taller than Chris, he was not much heavier. Paul's right arm draped over the top of his chair, while his left hand gestured as he spoke. Paul had an air of confidence about him. It was almost as if he were still in uniform, complete with Captain's bars. It was fitting. Just like the war: Captain talking to Sergeant.

Chris liked Paul. He was a good Captain and had treated Chris and his men like real people. As Paul continued, Chris could feel the positivity and authority that Paul exuded. Oh, Paul was a little more academic than Chris liked, but then his intellect fit well with his looks: wavy hair and wire-rimmed glasses. They had made a good team in Nam. *We would still make a good team now.*

"Are you with me, Chris, or am I in this by myself?" Paul shifted, putting both feet on the floor, both forearms out in front of him on the table. The drink in one hand, his eyes staring right into Chris'.

Chris looked right back, silent for ten long seconds; a pause that seemed like minutes. His eyes, although still looking at Paul, lost focus, and everything became a blur of colors. He, too, took a trip back to Nam – the senseless loss of life, the knowledge that there was no way to win, the fact that Washington wouldn't let them win even if they could have.

"Count me in," he blurted out before he was completely recovered from his thoughts. Then, as if he had never said them, he repeated, "Count me in."

"Good." Paul was satisfied, for now. His eyes lit up with approval. Chris would be an excellent partner. Together they could do much more than either alone. They complimented each other well, both being intelligent and savvy in different ways. Paul more the academician, while Chris had more of the street smarts. Paul was a little more thorough, Chris a little more reckless. Paul had the power of verbal persuasion, while Chris was more physically gifted. In each area, they

8

were closely matched with just a slight edge one way or the other.

"Just one thing, Chris. Somebody *is* going to pay, but nobody gets hurt. I've had all the violence I can stand in a lifetime."

"Agreed. I thought you would feel that way."

Catching the waitress' attention, Paul motioned her over. "What'll it be, Chris? It's on me."

"I'll take a Bud." The waitress gave a slight affirmative nod and flounced away.

"How would you like that for your housekeeper?" asked Paul as he motioned to the departing waitress.

"No thanks," smiled Chris. "Haven't had much time for chicks since I got back. Even moved out of my old man's house. Got a little apartment on the other side of the city. Needed time to think and, well, you know."

"Yes, things are different all over. Friends gone, some married, some just different. I don't know, maybe it's just me. I'm four years older than when I left, physically, anyway. Here, let me pay for the beer. Keep the change." Paul unfolded two bills and placed them on the edge of their table. "Where was I? Oh, yeah, four years older physically, but seems like ten mentally. You know, the things I thought were so important before, don't seem so important now. In fact, a lot of it seems, what would you say, false, meaningless, pretentious, plastic? You know what I mean."

Chris was listening and thinking how much alike they were. Feeling many of the same things Paul was talking about, Chris had spent many hours in his apartment thinking along those lines. And, about how unfair it was that old politicians could send vibrant young people into war, tearing up their lives and families. Then, there was the hovering cloud of guilt. *How is it that I'm still here instead of Jess and Bill?*

"Yeah, you know it, Paul. It's like we've been thinking the same thing, and now we can stop thinking and start doing."

"Well, not completely," Paul replied. "We can start doing, but we can't stop thinking. One thing for sure, whatever we do it's going to cost money – a lot of money. If we want to publish a magazine, do lobbying, search for MIA's, or whatever, it'll take money."

"Don't look at me," said Chris with a shrug of his good-sized shoulders. "I don't have any."

"Neither do I, but you know who does?"

"Lots of other people."

"Where do they keep their money?" asked Paul.

"In a sock?"

"Yeah, funny guy, in a sock. Well, I was thinking *banks*. In fact, on the plane on the way home, I was even then thinking of the two of us and various talents we have that could be utilized in an operation of this sort."

"What did you come up with?" asked Chris as he drained the last of his Bud and leaned back in his chair, his feet out front and crossed at the ankles, his strong fingers intertwined and rested on his midsection.

"I've come up with a simple plan. One that fits us just right. I'll rough it out for you now, then we can take our respective parts home and do some polishing."

"Tell me more."

"Well, my father's an architect, and I'm going to be working with him. Since I graduated from the U, he's willing to let me take additional responsibility. Your father is a building contractor specializing in light commercial construction – churches, small schools and office buildings,

10

right?"

"Right."

"What could be more natural? We'll bid some small bank jobs to do the architectural work. I'll get put on the project and design a weak link somewhere around the vault. I'll slip that sheet into the plans that are used on the job. Your firm gets the construction bid, you get put on as foreman and see that the weak link I design gets built in. Nobody's the wiser. After we get three or four built we can open them whenever the time is right. The war is not yet over in Nam and it's not over in the U.S. either. What do you think?"

Chris had moved so he was sitting on the edge of his chair, his hands still folded together, only now his fingers were white where they met. His eyes focused straight ahead at Paul as he reviewed the plan. Chris realized he had been staring at Paul so intently that he'd forgotten where he was. He looked quickly away, sweeping the scene he found himself in – a nice hotel lounge, soft chairs and cold drinks. Thirty minutes ago he came to meet an Army buddy, and now he was all set to participate in robbing a bank. *A bank? Three or four banks! What the hell was going on?*

"I think we can do it, should do it, and will do it!" There was no lack of conviction in Chris' voice as he thought about the fat cats in Washington who had murdered his comrades in arms. "We've got to take our time," Chris continued. "We've got to lay the groundwork right. If either of us appears too eager it could easily raise suspicions. We've got a lifetime to do it, so let's each do a little more planning and meet again." Even as he said this, Chris started doubting whether he would have the will to wait as long as it seemed the plan was going to take.

"Good point, Chris. Another thing, not many people around here know that we know each other as well as we do. We should keep it that way. Let's meet in unfamiliar places, changing locations and calling each other as seldom as possible. I don't want to meet your friends or relatives or know who they are, and I don't want you to meet my people. The fewer people who know about the two of us the better."

"Right," Chris replied, "the FBI could piece things together later if a lot of people know about our relationship. Give me a couple days, Paul, then you call and set up a meeting. Here's my number at my new apartment."

Chris handed Paul a slip of paper with his left hand and reached with his right for a handshake as they both rose to leave.

"You think it over Chris, I want you to be sure about this one way or another by our next meeting. Take it easy now, okay?"

"Yeah, see ya."

Paul sat back down and stared at Chris' back as he strode away. *If anybody can do it*, Paul thought, *Chris can.*

2

JANUARY 1973
MEETING

"Watch out! Slow down! Take it easy," Paul said to himself out loud, as he drove to downtown Minneapolis. It was January 25th, snowy and slippery. *Four years away and I've forgotten how to drive on snow*, he mused. Actually, the scene was beautiful. Big snowflakes fell straight down creating a kind of winter wonderland. *Funny how you miss things when you're gone.* It made Paul feel warm inside. *Being back home again feels good!*

The anticipation of a special lunch meeting added to his good feeling. Two days ago he and Chris had met, and now this. Paul parked his '72 Buick Riviera, locked the doors and started walking half a block to the restaurant. A quick glance at his watch showed that he was 15 minutes early to his 11:45 luncheon date. Well, it really wasn't *a date*, but he was excited nonetheless.

Paul's mother was a steady customer at a Nicollet Mall dress shop called "The Empress," and was well acquainted with the owner, Mrs. Thoms. Mrs. Thoms owned ten dress shops in the Twin Cities area. Through her, Paul's mother had gotten to know a younger woman named Ellen Nantucket, the merchandise buyer and assistant supervisor for the stores. Ellen had been in the University Chorus with Paul while attending the U. Paul and Ellen had become casually acquainted with each other, but they did get along well the time or two they had been at the same parties.

Paul's mother had mentioned to Mrs. Thoms that Paul was back from Vietnam. Ellen had overheard and remarked how she would enjoy visiting with Paul about the old days. Paul's mother casually relayed this information to Paul, and here he was, going downtown in the snow to meet her.

The heavy, wet snowflakes kept landing on Paul's glasses giving him a distorted view ahead. *Let 'em fall.* It was gorgeous. The wet flakes covering the fire hydrants, dirty streets, asphalt parking lots, and the parked cars made a storybook scene. It was about 30 degrees, but he didn't feel chilled at all.

Ellen, he was remembering, was a sharp, attractive woman with a childlike exuberance and freshness. She was not somebody you would seek out at a party, but when you were with her, she made you feel special. She was that kind of person. But, what about now? At this time, four years later, Paul found himself thinking of her with a lot of intensity. *What has she been doing socially? Why did she say she would like to see me? Maybe she was just trying to humor my mother. Why have I got the butterflies? Let's see, it's just 11:45. I'm right on time.*

Inside the Nicollet Mall restaurant, Ellen had found a table for two where she could watch the door. Her cup of coffee gave up slow motion swirls of steam under her gaze. She had purposely arrived fifteen minutes early to give herself time to think.

She was not comfortable at all. A kind of uneasiness pervaded her entire being. *What am I doing in this situation anyway? Sure, I knew who Paul Grayson was at the U...though he was a year or two ahead of me. Yes, I happened to get to know his mother through work at the store, and through her I've kept track of him.* She remembered when she found out Paul Grayson was in Vietnam from his mother at the store. It became their small talk topic. One day she realized she was truly interested in his well-being, and it was for her own interest she followed his locations and activities during his tours. She had even sent Paul a Christmas card the last two years.

She searched her heart and mind, trying to find the source of her uneasiness. Was it because seeing Paul would bring back painful memories of her brother, Steve? No, painful as that was, she had learned to confine those feelings mostly to her private moments. Maybe it was the feeling of being out of her league. Ellen recalled the same feeling during her university days when she'd been invited to a couple of choral gatherings that included Paul Grayson and his friends. They had an easy grace with money. They handled and talked about money in such a casual way. There was never any doubt for them about having enough for anything they wanted.

Ellen didn't blame them. They didn't know any different. She did. Her parents were killed in a tragic automobile accident and had left her and Steve with just a small insurance settlement. He was 17 and she just 16 at the time, and she learned the value of money in a hurry. From then on, she felt a sort of resentment towards anybody who didn't share the same regard for the value of money. Maybe it wasn't real resentment, but it probably accounted for the uneasiness she felt now as she waited for someone from an affluent family.

I wonder what Paul is like now, she thought, as she placed both elbows on the table, brought both hands up and rested her chin on her intertwined fingers. At the university, he was popular with most everybody. He seemed to have a genuine interest in people and was polite, yet firm in his dealings with those around him. She remembered how, at one chorus party, he had bodily thrown out one of the tenors

15

who had too much to drink and was pestering the girls, especially her. He had even asked her for a date, which she had turned down. She had felt a strong inferiority among the affluent then, although not so much now. It was probably a minor scene to him and doubted he'd even remember it. *How would he remember me?* she wondered.

"Ellen? Ellen Nantucket?" The question startled her back to the present.

"Yes, Paul, it's nice to see you," she said hesitantly, as she slid her chair back, its legs screeching on the tile floor, and stood up. She extended her hand to him while quickly scanning him. The good-looking college boy she remembered had been replaced by a mature, handsome man. Although, the same self-assurance seemed present.

"Ellen, thanks so much for accepting this luncheon date," Paul replied as he took her hand. "Please, sit down." Paul was pleased with what he saw. Ellen was even more attractive than he remembered. The transition from college girl to woman had enhanced her. That rare sparkle was present in her eyes and her smile had a disarming warmth. *She must be about 5'-8"*, thought Paul, *but it's hard to tell, as she is so well-proportioned.* Of course, working in a dress shop meant she was dressed very stylishly. Her radiant face was framed by the most beautiful, shiny black hair.

"My mother tells me," Paul started, "you are a buyer for the Empress Dress Shop at Nicollet Mall. My mother probably keeps your business going strong," he laughed.

"Yes, I've worked there full time for three years now. I also do some supervising at some of our other store locations. Mrs. Thoms has ten dress shops in the Twin Cities. I also worked there part time while going to the U – when we weren't on a chorus tour, that is. I'm sure you remember those tours. Paul, what about you? I know you just got back from Vietnam. What are your plans?"

"Would you care for a cocktail?" inquired the waitress who swooped in from out of nowhere. Paul motioned to Ellen and lifted his eyebrows.

"No thanks, I go back to work in half an hour. Mrs. Thoms might not appreciate a tipsy buyer," laughed Ellen.

"No thanks," said Paul, "me neither. Just leave us the menu. Ellen, I'm buying—you have anything you want."

"Thanks, Paul, but I prefer Dutch treat today. Really."

Paul was going to protest but as their eyes met he read a message he didn't quite understand. "Sure, Ellen, let's order so you're not late for work."

Their orders were taken and the conversation continued. "What about you, as I was asking before we were so rudely interrupted," she laughed.

"Well, first, I'm just going to bum around for a week or so, but my father wants me to work with him. I graduated with a degree in architecture, and he'd like me to get enough experience to pass the test, and eventually, I suppose, take over the firm. My father started this architectural firm back in the early '50s, and he's built it into a fair-sized operation. He'd like to see it remain in the family, and, right now, I don't have any better plans so...." He shrugged.

"Sounds great. I'm sure you will do well at it." Their food arrived quickly, and small talk continued through the meal. When they had finished eating and were finishing coffee, a kind of silence fell on them. As often happens, the awkward silence caused both of them to start speaking at the same time.

"Well, I better..."

"It's nice that..."

Paul smiled a warm smile at Ellen as she laughed quietly and waved him ahead.

"Go ahead," she laughed. "What is it?"

"Just was thinking how glad I am that my mother shops in your store," laughed Paul, "and how glad I am you agreed to spend your lunch hour with me." He was leaning forward now and looking right into her eyes. "In four years away from home, a lot has changed, and a person doesn't really fit in like before. The old friends have changed, married, divorced, moved, interests change, or whatever. It's like starting all over. And, if I have to start over, this is a nice way to do it."

Ellen was a little uneasy under Paul's gaze, yet it felt good. Paul was certainly sincere. A very nice man. Flashing a sheepish half smile, she replied, "I better be getting back. My lunch hour is almost gone. It's been fun, Paul, thanks. Thanks a lot."

"Ellen, I don't know that much about you," Paul offered, "so if I'm out of line just say so. I'd like to see you again, soon. Could we have dinner sometime? Then we'd have all the time we wanted to talk. You're a good listener, and, well, I could use someone to help program me back into this world."

"You've probably got so many homecoming parties and get-togethers with your friends, Paul, I won't be of much help."

"No, not really. Oh my folks have organized a get-together with some of the old gang, but it's not the same. They're from my old world – you're from my new. What do you say?"

"Well..." she wavered, as her gaze met his enthusiastic eyes.

"Good. How about tomorrow night?"

"Tomorrow? Thursday? Okay, if you're sure you..."

"I'll pick you up at 8:00, okay?"

Ellen waited at the door as Paul took her money and his and paid at the cash register.

"Here's your dollar and 52 cents change," Paul said as he extended his hand and gave her a mock frown.

"Thanks," she said as she pretended not to notice his frown and raised her nose slightly. They both looked at each other and laughed as they left the restaurant.

Outside, the snow had continued to fall in large, lazy flakes. The outlines of hidden benches and cars were much softer than when they had entered the restaurant. There was a tangible gentleness around them that entered into their emotions. They could feel it, especially Paul. It was like a holy pause. *When you've been in Nam, you can appreciate this feeling more than most people,* he reflected.

"I'll walk you to your store to make sure no harm befalls you on your way."

"That's not necessary, but since you insist!" Ellen's voice had an extra dimension to it. She was usually bright and cheerful anyway, but now it had an even brighter tone. Paul offered his arm and Ellen took it. They walked the short distance in silence, taking in the winter beauty. With each step, fresh snow crunched beneath their feet. The storefront came into view, and they stopped at the double doors at the entrance.

"Well, this is it. Back to the grindstone. Thanks Paul."

"Remember, tomorrow at 8:00," said Paul. "Good-bye."

Paul turned to go back to his car, and Ellen opened the door to go into the store. Paul had taken just a couple steps when he whirled around. "Ellen!" he called. "Ellen, wait up!"

"What is it?" she said, as she stepped back outside.

"Man, I almost forgot," he said breathlessly. "I don't know where you live."

"Oh," she looked into his serious face and started laughing. "Wouldn't that be something," she said between laughs. "I'd be sitting home waiting for you and you'd be driving around looking for me!"

Paul started laughing too. "To think I was a Captain in the Army. My strategy here sure was incomplete."

"I've got an apartment in Bloomington. Here, let me write my address and phone number on a piece of paper. Come in the store, Paul, would you? I'll get a pencil and paper. You can meet Mrs. Thoms, too."

The store was a mid-sized women's store dealing in fashions for the over forty affluent set. This store also served as headquarters for the other stores in the area. Paul followed Ellen past the cash register and up three steps to the office area in back. Mrs. Thoms looked up from her desk.

"Mrs. Thoms, I'd like you to meet Paul Grayson – Mrs. Grayson's son? You know, the one just back from Vietnam."

Mrs. Thoms was a large, portly woman in her late 50's, guessed Paul. She had the characteristic look and mannerisms of an affluent lady. As Ellen spoke to her, she removed her diamond studded glasses and let them hang by the ruby chain she had around her neck, then turned to Paul. "Paul Grayson, Marcie Grayson's son?"

"Yes, that's right Ma'am."

"Well, it's certainly nice to meet you, young man. I'm sure your mother is glad to have you home safe and sound. A lot of young men never made it back home..." her voice trailed off as she glanced at Ellen returning from her desk with a piece of paper for Paul.

"Nice meeting you, Mrs. Thoms, I've got to be going now." Ellen was leading the way back down the steps.

"Say hello to Marcie for me, won't you?" shouted Mrs. Thoms.

"Is she as snobby as she seems?" Paul whispered.

"Oh, she's quite a nice lady once you get to know her. She had no children, her husband died many years ago, so I'm kind of like a daughter to her. It works out well for both of us. Maybe I can tell you more about it sometime."

They had reached the door, and Paul turned to her. "Ellen, thanks again, for a nice day. See you tomorrow. Bye."

"Bye," said Ellen, waving her hand slightly. "Bye."

As Paul was retreating down the sidewalk, Ellen stood at the door staring at his back, but seeing something altogether different.

He looks and acts a lot like Steve, she thought. *I wonder if Steve would have*...her thoughts trailed off as she wiped away a tear that had made its way to her rosy cheek. She turned away from the door. Though her eyes were misty, she'd have no trouble finding her office. She'd done it many times before under similar conditions.

3

JANUARY 26, 1973
DATE NIGHT

"Paul, that was neat, really neat, eating with no shoes on. I almost singed my eyebrows when she put a flame to my supper," laughed Ellen.

"I told you you'd like that Japanese restaurant," Paul said brightly, as he braked to a slippery stop at the traffic light. "I always enjoy the Fuji-yu." Paul glanced at Ellen just in time to see her smile fade slightly, then recover quickly.

"It's the first time I've been there. I guess my enthusiasm seems a little naive to you. Sounds like you're a regular. Probably no big deal to you."

"Not at all, Ellen," said Paul as he continued to navigate the snow covered streets of Minneapolis. "Haven't been there in four years. I really enjoyed it mostly because you were with me. You're so positively optimistic – it makes me feel good. You're a boost to my attitude." Paul gave Ellen a full look and his best smile. Ellen returned the smile and slid over towards Paul on the bench seat, put both her hands around his right upper arm and clasped them lightly together. She rested her head momentarily on Paul's right shoulder, then sat up again to observe traffic. It was almost a sisterly gesture, almost, but not quite.

They drove in silence for a while – not an uncomfortable silence, more of a reflective, anticipating silence. "I'm glad you agreed to come over to the house, Ellen, it'll be enjoyable just to sit and be. You're easy

22

to be with. I appreciate that."

"Well, I do know your mother, Paul, and I've met your father a time or two when he's stopped in the shop for your mother. So, I'm not a complete stranger."

"Something I didn't tell you," laughed Paul, as he turned in the driveway, "is nobody's home. Both of them have a meeting this evening. Talk about luck!"

"Paul, you little rascal!" Ellen mocked as Paul got out of the Buick and went around to open her door.

"Never fear, Paul is here." They both laughed as Paul took Ellen's arm to lead her up the winding walk to the large front entrance of the Grayson's large, Southern Colonial home. Three majestic Doric columns stood as silent sentinels on each side of the entrance.

Inside the front hall was dark. The large evergreens in the yard that flanked the front walk cast a shadow from the outdoor lighting. As Paul turned to shut the door, he momentarily wondered if he should reach for the light switch, or Ellen.

As the light came on, Ellen turned a complete circle letting her eyes adjust to the light. "Wow, this is impressive, Paul. I—I feel out of place." *Why did I say that*, thought Ellen. *I've got to get over that feeling. It's time I enjoyed what is. Not what could be or should be. Okay. Give it a try.* "Paul, bear with me. I didn't mean you are making me feel out of place. I mean, it's a house like I've never been in before. It's large and very tastefully decorated, at least what I can see from here."

"I'll show you around, Ellen. By the way, I'd feel out of place, so-to-speak, at your place, too. A person always feels more comfortable in familiar settings, as you know. Let me take your coat and put it in the

23

hall closet. Ahead, my lady, you see the grand staircase," he said formally, adding a sweeping gesture as he looked at Ellen rather than the staircase he was pointing out.

"Paul, I thought this was only in the movies! I..."

"Then to my right," interrupted Paul, in his best tour guide voice, "is my father's sanctuary—his library—probably locked," mocked Paul as he tried the knob. "Yes, thought so. Take a peek to your left. Ta da! The royal kitchen."

Ellen caught a glimpse of a rather austere, clinical looking kitchen as Paul took her elbow and ushered her through it into a thickly carpeted room full of cabinets – obviously the formal dining room.

"This is..."

"Don't tell me...it's the dining room," Ellen said with false amazement. "But really, that chandelier and heavy oak table...wow! Just great!"

Passing through the large living room, Paul continued the tour upstairs showing Ellen the bedrooms and his mother's extra-large dressing room/closet. "Recognize any of those dresses?" Paul winked.

"Now to my favorite area – saving the best till last and all that. Come," said Paul, as he took Ellen by the hand and led her through a doorway off the kitchen into another heavily, paneled medium-sized room.

This room looked like a den or a family room, and the carpet felt very plush under Ellen's feet.

"I dreamed this area up when I was in Nam and my parents had it done before I got back. The door over there leads to my bedroom and bath. I can live at home for a while, but still have my privacy. What do you think?"

24

Ellen, still holding Paul's hand, was looking around slowly. Paul had used the dimmer switch to keep the lights at a low level. Off to her right was a large fireplace with large grey stones and a heavy, rustic wood mantle that looked like it had come out of an old English castle. The ceiling had large wooden beams spanning across the room with a white stucco effect between the beams. The other walls were done in a beautiful, cherry wood plank, with a large curtain in the center of the wall opposite the fireplace.

As she was looking at the curtain, Paul, reading her thoughts, interjected, "That is a sliding glass door that leads to a private courtyard area, which is just a jump from the backyard pool. It's also my private entrance. Anyway, it's too cold out there, which reminds me—you sit right here," Paul said, as he guided Ellen to a velvety couch near the fireplace. "You can even put your feet up on the footstool," Paul lightly laughed as he pushed an obviously expensive hassock into position. "I'm going to get a little fire going. Just sit back and relax." Ellen returned Paul's broad smile a little reservedly, that old out-of-place feeling rearing its ugly head.

Paul expertly placed logs on the fireplace grate, resting on his haunches to do so. Ellen observed Paul's broad back which narrowed down to his slim waist, his coal black hair neatly combed and styled. An attractive man, she thought, in more ways than one. *Wish I could relax!*

"There, that should give us a warm cheery fire in just a few minutes. I'll be right back." Paul left the room and shut the door.

Ellen's gaze was drawn to the ever increasing flames. Paul had turned the light off on his way out so the only light was the flickering light of the fire. The clear outline of the flames faded as her eyes focused on a distance much farther away. *His broad back, narrow hips, wavy hair—Steve's was blond, thank goodness, or this would be too weird.* Paul's mannerisms, even the way he was crouched before the fire was just like Steve. *Man, it's almost four years now*, thought Ellen, that Steve had told her he was joining the Air Force. *It seems like yesterday sometimes and an eternity other times.*

Steve and Ellen had always been close. They were the only two children of Keith and Ruth Nantucket. Even so, they got along unusually well for brother and sister. Then came that terrible stormy, slippery night in November of 1966 when both their parents were killed in a grinding, head-on collision. From then on, Steve and Ellen clung together as they successfully fought the efforts of outsiders to separate them or to force them to live with an unkindly aunt and uncle.

Ellen adored her older brother. Steve, was a very mature young man and responded well to the challenge brought on by the death of their parents. He was like a father to Ellen at times, but mostly he was the model older brother most girls dream of.

When Steve told Ellen he had joined the Air Force, she was not surprised. She had a part-time job and was headed for college, so he was free to go. He had talked about serving his country and also about being a pilot someday. This seemed like the chance to do both. Yet, it happened fast. A tearful farewell as Steve went to basic training. A tearful welcome home after basic. Then, to flight school. Then a tearful farewell as Steve left for his first tour in Vietnam. They shared a two-week get together in Japan. Steve was on leave and Ellen had finished a university choir tour of Japan.

Then, the bombshell: killed-in-action. She remembered the disbelief, the unwillingness to face the truth, and the pain of knowing Steve's body was buried by the enemy without love or care. The doctors, shots, medication, counseling, some here, some in Japan, it all seemed a dream. But, it enabled her to become functional again. The release of emotion, the rebuilding of her life after loss, again. Still the pain was there, very near the surface.

Suddenly, coming back to the present, Ellen realized her face was teary. Just as she reached into her purse she realized Paul was standing at the end of the couch with two wineglasses.

"Looks like you could use this," said Paul, extending the glass to her.

"No, I...well, yes, thanks," replied Ellen, accepting the wine. "How...how long have you been standing there?"

"Just got here, but I can see something is wrong. Is it something I've done?"

"No, not at all – not directly anyway. Nothing you could help either." Ellen smiled briefly as she tried to dab at her eyes and nose. "Look at me, ruining what has been a perfectly marvelous evening, at least for me."

Paul set his wine glass down on the end table and crossed in front of Ellen, sitting down and forward on the couch while putting an arm around her shoulder and one hand on her forearm. "Ellen, the evening is definitely not ruined and I've had an extraordinary, enjoyable evening. But something is really bothering you. Now, I don't know you very well or what's been happening in your life, so I can't help unless you let me. Share your problem with me. I've been thinking of myself too much. It's about time I get with it. You're helping me, maybe I can help you," said Paul softly.

Ellen grabbed another tissue, wiped up a bit, took a deep breath and said, "I guess I owe you that much. You don't need my troubles, but as long as you asked..." Ellen repeated about her parents' death and her life with Steve, and then about Steve's untimely death, and finally how much Paul resembled Steve, except, thank goodness, for the hair color.

All the while Paul sat back in the couch looking straight ahead with a grim look on his face. Ellen occasionally glanced at Paul, but mostly sat with her hands folded in her lap clutching a tissue. When she finished she was crying again.

"Paul, this is awful, I'm a wreck. Where can I freshen up?" Paul directed her to his bathroom. Then he placed two more logs on the fire and went to the cabinet and took out his guitar.

After a few warm-up chords he was playing his old favorites. The fire warmed the bottoms of his feet which were resting on the leather hassock. He was slouched down on the couch humming along with the chords when Ellen came back. She stopped in the doorway and returned Paul's gaze. The flickering shadows hid any evidence of her tears and played softly on her exquisite features. Just like a doll, Paul thought, a very appealing doll!

"I didn't know you played," Ellen said softly. "It sounds nice. Real nice. Go on."

Paul said nothing, but looked at a spot next to him on the couch. Ellen caught on and sat down beside him while Paul played on, lightly humming an old standard. Soon Ellen joined in, harmonizing with Paul as they sang a couple of numbers popular in the 60's.

"Oh, Paul, this is fun," laughed Ellen as she caught her breath after a particularly fast number. "In addition to the university choir, I went on tour with the All-American Touring Chorus one summer way back when. Boy, I haven't sung like this since then. You do real well, Paul."

"Hey, this *is* fun. You can really harmonize...for a girl," he laughed.

"Sing and play, you bet. My mother wanted me to learn to play concert piano and sing opera, so we compromised. I took voice lessons for a while to make her happy, and she let me take guitar lessons. Didn't learn that much, but enough to strike a few chords around the ol' campfire."

Paul had moved to a sitting position on the couch's edge as the playing and singing got more serious, while Ellen had settled against the couch back in a semi-slouched, relaxed position. Conversation stopped as they both remained in position looking at each other. Paul's face glowed from the fire's light, the flames softly reflected in his glasses. Ellen's face was half shadowed by Paul's muscular frame. Paul lifted the guitar up over his head with his left hand and his eyes momentarily left Ellen as he leaned to the left to set the guitar down.

Quickly he turned back to Ellen, whose eyes had not left him. Slowly he leaned forward, heart beating faster, with fear yet purpose. Ellen did not move. His lips lightly touched hers. Stayed. Retreated. Ellen had offered no resistance, yet no encouragement. Paul's face was about a foot away from Ellen's, both looking deeply into the other's eyes. The only sound was the snapping and crackling of the fire.

Ellen broke the silence. "Paul, try that again," she said quietly.

Paul leaned forward to place his lips on Ellen's. At first, with a light touch, then as Ellen responded, more urgency. Ellen's arms had gone around Paul and pulled him into a tight embrace. Ellen removed her lips from his and buried her head on his shoulder, not letting up on her bear hug. Paul responded by holding her tight. Finally the awkward position on the couch dictated they move. Paul stood up in front of Ellen and held out both hands to her. She accepted and he pulled her up into another embrace. Ellen responded again, but only shortly, before she took her lips from his and placed her cheek next to his, continuing to hold him. Paul stroked her hair slowly and gently as they remained this way for several minutes.

"Paul, I've got to go," said Ellen. She slowly broke away, lowering her hands to around his waist, and then letting them follow his outstretched arms, then hands, then nothing. "It's been a lovely time. I haven't felt like this for a long time. It's a little confusing to me. I..."

"Your coat," interrupted Paul, "I'll get it and we'll drive you home." Paul's voice had a happy lilt to it.

"Paul, I hope you don't think I'm upset, I mean, asking to go home and all," Ellen stated, as soon as Paul returned with her coat.

"Not at all. It's kind of late. We can talk in the car."

"Thank you," Ellen replied cautiously, then quickly she danced up on her tiptoes and gave Paul a quick kiss on the cheek before he knew what was happening. "Thank you," she said with a sparkle in her voice.

Slipping their shoes on and stepping outside, they were greeted by a still, cold, crisp, clear night; the kind of night that foretells a cold, cold day. The stars were brilliant through the crystal cold sky. Sounds traveled for miles on nights like these, but it was very quiet now. Ellen walked several steps ahead of Paul as he turned to pull the heavy colonial door closed behind them. She exhaled deeply, creating a small cloud of steamy breath while maintaining her two-step lead. She had her door partly open before Paul could perform the usual courtesy. He held the door for her and gently closed it as she slid across the seat.

As they started out the driveway, Paul was honoring Ellen's unspoken request for quiet. Ellen was trying to sort things out in her own mind. *Paul is so much like Steve*, she thought , *maybe too much. Am I attracted to him because of this? I should get over Steve, it's been too long. No, I'll never ever get over him, but I have to get on with my life. Why did that damn war ever have to happen? I could still have Steve. Then I'd know what it is between Paul and me.*

"Ellen if you want to talk about something just say so, otherwise I'll wait."

"Thanks, I'll wait. Not ready. Not yet."

"When you're ready, I'll be here." His eyes locked on hers for an instant.

The rest of the ride was quiet. The moon was almost full and cast a golden white glow over the snowy country. Pretty. Picturesque. Moody.

Paul offered to walk Ellen to her door, but she politely but firmly refused. Paul was beginning to understand her more. Not enough, but more. Ellen took his hand and gave it a quick squeeze, and was gone.

4

FEBRUARY 1973
CHRIS & PAUL

"Chris, why don't you move back in with me and Rita? I'd sure like that." The question asked by Chris' father, Matt, lacked real conviction. The elder Stone had asked the same question for the last five working days in a row, in fact, starting with the day after Chris had moved to an apartment of his own. The question had become more of a greeting than a question. *Rita?* He had met her, but barely knew her.

Matt and Chris met each morning in the construction shack: Chris just for someplace to go in the morning for a few minutes and Matt to plan the activities for the day. Matt was a grizzled old veteran of the construction game, building the business from the ground up. It was never more than marginally successful, but it provided a focus for his life and a livelihood for his family.

"Pops, you know I'll be back when I've got things sorted out for myself. It's nothing personal." Matt cocked his hard hat back on his head, extended both weathered hands in front of him and leaned slightly forward until he came in contact with the drafting table. Spread before him were blueprints of their current project: a small office building. Matt assumed a posture of study, and Chris turned to observe him.

Chris had not told the whole truth when he said there was nothing personal in his moving out. Right now, he was looking

32

across the table at a man of action and decision. It's true, he was a good builder. However, Pops was a different man at work than on evenings and weekends. Why did it have to be so? After work, and shot after shot of whiskey, the old man was unbearable. The least irritation set him off on rants, tirades and verbal abuse. Chris had not known any different before the Army – it's just how life was. But, he knew better now. He didn't have to put up with it anymore.

Chris continued to observe as Matt mechanically reached in his shirt pocket for a cigarette, lit it, and started tracing his index finger over the blueprints. Chris had not really noticed his father's face since he got back from Nam. The lines and redness in his face and the surface blood vessels all told their story. Chris didn't like what he was seeing. *A lot of age for a man of just 55...*

"Pops," Chris broke in, "after you get the men going this morning, stop back in here. I want to talk to you, okay?"

It was Matt's habit to get to the construction site about 30 minutes ahead of his men to plan the day's work. Since Chris was going to work with his dad, at least for a while, he followed the same routine. It was just a few minutes before 8:00, and as Matt pulled a dusty, torn curtain aside, he noticed the men start to filter in. Reaching for the door handle and grinding his cigarette on the floor, Matt said, "Yeah, I'll get 'em started and be back." He paused for a second, gave Chris a full look, and then went out without saying anymore.

The door closed, and Chris was now alone in the shack. *Might as well take a load off,* he thought, and slid a chair toward a window that gave him a view of the building site. He turned the chair so he could sit down backwards, leaning his folded arms over the back of the chair. "What a good-sized man," Chris said aloud. "Why does he have to be this way!" As he looked out, his eyes and thoughts followed his father who moved across the makeshift gravel driveway towards the workers. Matt was a big, husky man, about 6'-2", solidly built, massive shoulders, with a full head of coal black hair tinged with gray. He wore an unzipped plaid jacket and tan coveralls with a hooded sweatshirt in between, all topped by his bright orange hard hat, his trademark.

Chris couldn't remember exactly when it was, maybe around age 12 or 13, but he'd never forget the episode. For some reason, Pops had come home in the middle of the afternoon on a Saturday. He usually spent all day at the corner bar, but not that day. Chris was watching a football game when Pops came storming in.

"Where's your mother?"

"I think she's grocery shopping."

"What the hell gives her the right to take off whenever she wants?" raged Matt.

Chris had moved forward on his chair and was watching the game less intently and his father more intently. He had seen Pops in this foul mood many times and it always led to no good.

"Son," he said, "if you ever find yourself a good woman, hang on to her. It'll be a miracle. Don't make the mistake I did. Ain't no woman worth her salt!"

If he said it once, he'd said it a hundred times, thought Chris. But, it always puzzled him. *What mistake?* His mother was a fine mother as far as he was concerned. Many times she had shielded him from the furies of his father. *Pops was scary.* Though only 13, he knew something of the world of girls his father was talking

34

about. And, as much as his mother meant to him, how would he ever find one better? *Who said you even had to get married?*

He remembered how his mother had come home with an armful of groceries and how Pops had berated her and finally struck her with a powerful backhand across her face. The blow knocked her to the floor, but she was up in an instant, with a thin trickle of blood coming from her nose and mouth. She had grabbed Chris by his hand, and, avoiding off-balance Pops, pushed Chris ahead of her, through the back door, and across the lawn to the Frasers.

He remembered how Mr. Fraser had gone to their house to talk to Pops and came back later to announce it was safe to go back home. When they did, he was gone. He didn't show up until the next afternoon, and when he did, Mr. Fraser came with Pops into the house. He looked very tired and defeated. They sent Chris to his room, but he could hear them talking anyway.

He could hear his father apologizing and talking to his mother in a way he hadn't heard from him before. He was pleading with her, which was highly unusual for Pops, to say the least. He also heard Pops tell her what a tremendous mother and wife she was. This was puzzling to Chris. *What?* All he had heard from Pops was what a poor woman she was, in every way.

Chris couldn't remember how many times some variation of this scene was repeated – three, maybe four times, but finally his mother was gone. Then, it was a succession of women: some stayed one night, one as long as six months. Some were good to Chris, some bad, some indifferent. Through them all he remembered, "There ain't no woman worth her salt."

He hadn't planned on working with his father, but Pops had been faithful about writing while Chris was away. *Got to give him that.* When he got his discharge, there was no place else to go. At first he was just going to hang around for a few days at home, then find some construction-related job in town. After his meeting with Paul a couple days ago, he decided to really get into his father's firm. That wouldn't be any problem, and *if Paul does his part*, thought Chris, *we've got a natural situation.*

"Pour us some coffee, will ya, Son?" bellowed Matt as he came through the door. Chris complied as Matt took off his hard hat and set it upside down on the table, wiping his brow with the back of his hand. "What is it, Son? What have you got on your mind?"

"Look, Pops," replied Chris hesitantly, "I know I told you before that I was going to be moving on in a few weeks. Well, I've changed my mind."

"Son, that's just great—we'll..."

"Pops, Pops, hold on a minute, will you? Let me finish, okay? I'd like to work with you, maybe even go into partnership. But first, I've got to find out if it'll work—you and me. Know what I mean?"

"Sure son, sure. I can see it now. Stone & Son Construction, hey..."

"Hold on, Pops, I'm not finished yet. Look, you've done a good job with the company, so this is no put-down. But, if it's going to support us both, we'll have to expand, take on a few more jobs. You'll have to be willing to let me do a couple jobs pretty much on my own, after I get some experience. I do the estimating, bidding, supervising – the whole works. You'll have to keep your nose out unless I ask for advice. I've got to find out if this is my thing before I get locked in."

36

"Son, that's no problem. We'll work together on this. It'll work out just fine, you'll see. When you wanna start for real?"

"I'll take the rest of the week and start on Monday, okay?"

"Sounds like a plan. Stay and finish your coffee, I've got to get back outside. Damn, it's cold. Hope we don't get a blizzard. We can handle the cold, but snow? That's different. See ya, Son." Matt opened the door to leave, ushering in a blast of cold air. Chris shivered. He wondered if it was from the cold outside or inside of him.

Chris was getting ready to leave when the door swung open, admitting another blast of cold air. A woman he didn't know hurried in rubbing her hands together, nodded at him, and headed for Matt's desk.

Taking her scarf and jacket off and throwing them carelessly across an empty chair, she turned to Chris and said, "And, you are?"

Chris was caught a bit off-guard as he looked at this older, attractive woman – 30's or 40's he guessed, nice, mousy blond hairdo with curls down to her shoulders, about 5'-7" or so, with a trim athletic body all packaged into an off-white ribbed sweater and tight, bell-bottom jeans. "Uh, I'm Chris Stone, and you are?"

"Oh, you must be Matt's son. I'm Harlow. I pick up the time cards every week and get the payroll ready for Friday. Will I be putting you on for this week?"

"No, I start next week, but I don't even know what my dad has planned for me. Better check with him. Actually, I'm getting ready to leave. Any questions?"

"Nope, I have to sit here a few minutes to review the timecards

37

in case I have questions while I'm still here. Nice to meet you." She leaned over and shook hands. "I guess I'll see you around." She gave him a nice smile as he left.

Randolph Grayson, prominent local architect, was slowly shuffling through a stack of papers atop his mahogany desk when Allen Stanton rapped quickly on the open door frame of his office. Putting the papers aside, he waved Allen in and motioned for him to sit. He looked down at his clasped, well-manicured hands and spoke. "Allen, I've called you into my office to talk about the future of my business. You've been with me since I started this company over 20 years ago. What I'm going to talk about must stay between you and me. And, I want you to be perfectly frank with me," Randolph said, with a serious tone. Looking up at his rotund business manager, he continued. "Paul has asked to join our firm with an eye to being a partner."

"Well, Randolph, he graduated university with a degree in architecture. He's an intelligent young man, a commissioned officer, and with some internship should be able to pass the exam."

"I know, I know—but something is different—I don't know what for sure. Most kids in college have the anti-establishment theme going. Paul never has, at least not that I know of." Randolph hesitated, then got up from his chair, turning to the inner office wall, pausing to look at the half dozen artist's renderings of some of his favorite projects, then continuing around to the window that overlooked Roberts Lake and Roberts Park.

"Go on, Randolph. You have more on your mind."

"You've been with me too long." He smiled quickly as he looked over at Allen, then turned back to continue his gaze outside. He made a striking figure. It was easy to see where Paul got his grace and good looks. Though 55, he was still a tall, well-built, athletic looking man. Silver gray hair along with the ever-present vested, gray pin-striped suit gave him the air of the successful businessman that he was.

"During the war, I noticed a shift in Paul's attitude through his letters and during his leave time back home. It wasn't the ranting, raving kind of change, but a more subtle shift of philosophy. I feel it even more now that he's been home a week or so."

"I wasn't aware of it at all," Allen offered, "but then I haven't seen much of him lately, either." He shifted his rimless glasses higher up on his shrew-like nose.

"It may be nothing, as I said, but this business takes a man who's 100 percent committed. Those people out there depend on me for a living," Randolph gestured to the outer offices. "We've built a solid reputation that we can't afford to tarnish. More importantly, if this isn't what Paul really wants to do with his life, it'll be a miserable existence for him, too."

"What do you want me to do?" asked Allen. "How can I help?"

"These reports you've brought in detail our financials, and Paul has asked to see them," he said as he raised a file folder with his left hand. "He's due in shortly, and I'd like you to stay here with us to go over the figures with him. You're a CPA and our business manager, so that will be natural, but more than that, watch for these things I've told you about. Be careful not to let my feelings prejudice you into seeing what's not there. I'm going to offer Paul a deal which will give him a year or two before he has to make up his mind about becoming a partner and possible successor to me. The plan would be for you to work closely with him for the next year. Question him, advise him, and get to know him. He'll probably tell you things he wouldn't tell me. If he is going to take over, the association he has with you will help him better understand the business side of running an architectural firm, and it'll help you understand him. If this isn't the right place for him, we'll all benefit by knowing about it." Randolph walked towards his desk, and added, "Remember Allen, this has to be confidential and you have to be frank with me." As he stood behind his desk, the intercom announced Paul's arrival.

"Send him in," responded Randolph. "Well, here we go!"

Paul came in and renewed acquaintances with Allen. After a little small talk, the three men looked over some of the financial data, then sat down in the two leather armchairs in the office, with Randolph behind his desk.

"Your father tells me you would like to join his firm," stated Allen.

Paul shifted a little uneasily under Allen's penetrating gaze. "Yes, we talked briefly about it a couple nights ago. I'd like to get something started now that the Army is behind me. I think it's time to get established, to embark on a career, so-to-speak." Paul laughed a little, somewhat strained.

"I think that's a good idea," countered Allen, humorless, glancing at Randolph. "Your father has built quite a business here as you've seen, and I know he would be proud to have you."

"That's right," answered Randolph, "and to get started, I've asked Allen for his ideas on how to do it in an accepted business fashion. What we'd like to do, Paul, is have you work with us for at least a year before we draw up any papers. Allen will work with you during this time. At the end of the year, we'll all sit down and see if it's in the best interest of all involved. I don't foresee any problems, Son, but this is new to you and I want to make sure this is something you can give your life to. Is that agreeable?"

"Sounds fair, Dad. But, I want to take on some responsibility fairly quickly, I want you to give me a job to handle—at least after we work together on a couple jobs. I want to work design, engineering, spec writing, drafting, bid letting, the whole works, with minimal supervision. Can you do that?"

"I don't know why not," answered Randolph, with a raised eyebrow toward Allen. "You know enough to ask for help if you need it, I presume."

"I hope so. I do know there is a lot I don't know and I'll need help. No doubt about that. It's just that I'll ask for help when I think I need it. I need to solve my own problems with minimal interference. Otherwise, I'll never find out if this is for me or not. Okay?" The three of them continued talking until Paul announced that he had an appointment downtown.

It was already 5:00, so he would have to hurry to make his 5:30 appointment with Chris. He had waited until the last minute for the meeting with his father since it was something he had not looked forward to. Now that it was over, he had a feeling of release. His father made him the kind of deal he expected. *He was always business – business this, business that.* Paul could remember how little his father shared life with him. How could he? He was always meeting with a client, working late on a project, attending a civic function...always something. He remembered how jealous he was when other fathers seemed to show up at class plays, basketball games and other activities.

But, not Randolph. He was always too busy. As a kid, Paul had more toys than anybody, and no shortage of anything. The envy of the neighborhood, he was the first kid with a motorcycle, first kid with his own car, first this, the most of that. Even so, it all had a hollow feel. Amongst all the material things, something still was missing. Now he knew. Maybe war did have a positive side. Most likely the good aspect of it was his growth: being away from home, growing older, being on his own, the responsibilities to his men as a Captain. *Loving, caring, sharing...that's what I've missed. And, it might not be too far away.* He smiled as he thought of Ellen, which caused a warm feeling inside. She was worth a smile anytime.

He realized how silly he must look walking to the "Last Round-up Bar" with a mile-wide grin on his face. The Last Round-up Bar was one of several along the sleazier part of Nicollet Avenue. Paul had chosen it because neither he nor Chris had ever been there before, nor would they probably ever be again. It was part of their plan not to be seen together by people who would know either of them.

The place was not very busy yet, so it was no problem finding a booth from where he could watch for Chris. Paul hadn't been in a country western bar before, so he was busy looking around at the cowboy and old west artifacts when Chris surprised him by slipping in the booth.

"Hey, Chris. How's it going?"

"Fine, man, real good. Hey, quite a meeting place you picked," mocked Chris, as he turned his head quickly to the left and panned the room, "but it's not your style."

"That's for sure," smiled Paul. "That's why I picked it. Nobody either of us knows is likely to be in here. That's the way we want it, remember?"

"Yah, no sweat, Paul. No sweat. Look, ah, how did it go at work for you? We still into this thing—you and me?"

Before Paul could reply, a cowgirl waitress came by to take their orders.

"A Bud."

"Make mine a Vodka and Seven." Paul's eyes narrowed a little as he sat back in the booth looking right into Chris' eyes. "I'm not sure I want to go through with this thing, Chris. I'm just not sure!"

"Hey, man!" replied Chris through clenched teeth. "You talk this thing up, lay it on me about Jess and Bill and the establishment and doing something to even the score. You get me thinking and planning, then you tell me you're going to bug out?" By now Chris was leaning forward onto the table with both hands clenched into fists. The cords on either side of his neck clearly stood out. "What the hell is this?" Chris continued in a loud whisper, "You telling me to make sure it's what *I* want!"

"Hold on, hold on," answered Paul in a loud, hoarse whisper, looking around. He had both hands in front with palms down, motioning Chris to hold it down. "I'm into this thing, okay? Take it easy. I just had to make sure about your feelings. This will never work if I have to drag you along. You've got to feel as deeply as I do about going through with this, and I think you just convinced me. We're into this together, all the way—no backing out."

43

Chris relaxed. "Yeah, so I got a little excited. You would too if you'd just made a deal with your old man to go into business with him, knowing you're just using him."

"I know how you feel," Paul replied. "I did the same thing. You know, it wasn't as easy as I thought it would be. I don't owe the ol' boy anything, yet when I was in his office talking to him, I could tell his business is his whole world. I wondered if what we're about to do will damage his business – even hurt him personally. At first I didn't care, but now I want to plan things so it doesn't reflect back on his firm. It'll make our job a lot tougher, but not impossible. I don't know how yet, but we'll need enough decoy bank jobs so it doesn't all trace back to our two firms. Let's work on that."

"It's strange that we live in two different worlds," observed Chris, "yet our experiences are very similar. For example, my old man gave me a rotten family life, yet watching him at work, he's giving it his best shot. He's contributing in his own way. Like you, at first I thought, what the hell, let the company go broke! Who cares? But, I know he does. And, now I do. Anyway," continued Chris, "if we plan carefully so that it doesn't get traced back to our businesses, we've isolated ourselves so *we* won't get caught and *they* won't get hurt."

"Sounds good," interrupted Paul. "The main purpose of our meeting tonight was to see if we want to go ahead, which we do, and to see if we both can make necessary arrangements within our companies to be in position to carry out our plans. Seems like we've accomplished that, so the next thing to do is to come up with some specific methods of operation. When do you start work?"

"I don't start 'til Monday. I wanted a few days."

44

"Good enough, me too. What do you say we get into the swing of our work for a couple weeks, then meet again? By then, we should have an idea of how much freedom and responsibility we really have to work with. We should know that before we come up with anything too specific."

"Yeah, okay, but I'm sure you've got some ideas."

"Well—yeah, that's true. In fact, let me tell you a little about what I have in mind so you can look for ways to make it work. It all starts with having the necessary drawings made up so that I can substitute my pages for the right ones when they assemble the blueprints being used at the construction site. We'll have to work on smaller, one-story banks, those with their vaults on the first floor, not in the basement. I would draw up counterfeit plans showing a roof vent or some such, over the corner of the vault. Only on the counterfeit drawings, it wouldn't look like it was over the vault. Of course, the section of roof over vaults are always made of reinforced concrete, but the extra reinforcing would be stopped short of totally covering the vault. Your part would be to see that the design flaw got properly constructed—or improperly, depending on your point of view."

"We'll both work on it over the next couple weeks," said Chris, as he drained the last of his beer. "Here's something else to be working on. Before any of this can happen, you've got to see that Stone Construction gets the contracts. That might not be so easy either."

"Not easy, but maybe not too hard. We'll see. My father has a good relationship with one of the wheels at the First American Bank System. They're always putting a bank up somewhere. We've

45

never worked on their smaller branch banks because they've been too small to monkey with. I'll put a word in to my father that something like that would be just my size."

"Paul, I've got to go. Call me in about two weeks, and we'll meet again. It's nice working with someone who knows the angles."

With a wave Chris was gone, leaving Paul in the booth to finish his neglected drink. A quick look at the Hamm's Beer clock on the wall reminded Paul it was about time for his date with Ellen. A busy day!

5

"Chris?"

"Yes..."

"Paul. Can you talk now?"

"Yeah, go ahead, nobody here."

"It's two weeks tonight. Can you meet?"

"Planned on it. Where?"

"Let's make it the lounge at the Vicksburg Hotel on the Bloomington strip. You know it?"

"Yeah, been by it a hundred times," replied Chris.

"Look, there's a chance I might have a problem making it, but I think I can, so let's say 7:30. If I'm not there by 7:45, check with the desk. About 20 percent chance I'll have to meet with a client, but I won't know till he calls sometime before 7:00 tonight. I don't think he will, but thought I'd warn you, okay?"

"Yep, that's okay, it's a good night for a drive. Are you working with your old man?"

"Yeah, about a week now. Haven't done anything but get acquainted with people and procedures. Tonight's potential client meeting would be my first, though I think it'll be an early morning meeting tomorrow. It's someone with plans for a small office building. How about you?"

"Same thing. Getting used to the operation. I think week after next I'll get my first job to handle, more or less by myself. Anyway, we can talk tonight. If you're not there by 7:45 or so I'll check with the desk. See you then."

Paul picked the Vicksburg on purpose. It was one of the new, larger hotels in the area, and nobody would notice two more people in the busy lounge. The Vicksburg had both a lounge and a restaurant, and the two were separated from each other by the lobby and a coffee shop. This was strategic, because Paul had arranged a date with Ellen for 8:30 in the Southern Room: the restaurant in the hotel's other wing.

Paul had seen Ellen twice since their first date – once for a movie in downtown Minneapolis, and once a play at the Guthrie. Each time it was coffee afterwards, then Ellen would go home. They enjoyed each other's company and were not rushing their relationship. In fact, they were more like friends than possible lovers. Paul knew that Ellen was having trouble handling Steve's death, so he stepped back. So again, two friends were going to have a late dinner. Ellen would just be getting back from some trouble-shooting at one of the nearby stores, so she would be in the area already. Paul had also explained the possibility he would have a client meeting and instructed her to check with the desk when she got there, around 8:30.

Paul knew he was taking a small risk, because he and Chris did not want to be seen together by anyone who knew either of them, but the layout at the Vicksburg made a chance meeting almost impossible. *In fact*, thought Paul, *I'll see Chris to his car, get in mine and drive around to the restaurant door and go in from there*. First class.

Paul continued with straightening his office. The new furniture and equipment had finally been delivered that morning, and now he was organizing the office to his satisfaction. The chrome chairs with orange vinyl and the sleek, modern black desk contrasted sharply with the

48

worn, heavy oak of his father's office two doors down the hall. Paul didn't particularly like this style, it was okay, but had done it to test his father. He wanted to see if his father would let him truly choose even his own office furniture. He had. *I shouldn't be surprised*, mused Paul. Ol' Randolph was pretty good at delegating authority, provided the recipient could handle it. *I guess I have to handle it.*

"Paul, Paul, oh, there you are. You have a call, you'll have to take it at my desk. Your own phone should be installed tomorrow." Gwen, the attractive young receptionist, led Paul to the phone.

"That's the way it goes," remarked Paul as he turned to hang up the phone while sitting on the edge of Gwen's desk.

"What's the matter?" Gwen smiled.

"My first appointment with a client," frowned Paul, "and I should be happy as a lark. Only now I've got to cancel another..." Paul's voice trailed off as he smiled at Gwen. "And what do you care?" Paul said in a kidding manner as he picked up the phone to make a couple of calls before heading for his office. Gwen was gathering her things getting ready to leave. He waved her out the door and said, "See you tomorrow." In mid-dial, he glanced at his watch. "Gwen, wait up," he set the phone down. "Why are you here so late?"

"I, ah, I had to do some catching up, being the new girl and all."

"Well, have a good night." He continued getting his office ready until it was time to leave for his client meeting.

At 7:15 Chris pulled into the parking lot at the Vicksburg. He wasn't sure where the lounge was and wanted to be on time for the meeting. Halfway through his second beer he noticed it was close to 8:00 and no Paul. He told the waitress he'd be right back as he headed

49

for the front desk a short distance away.

"Yes, we have a message for Chris Stone. Let's see, ah—here it is."

"Thanks," said Chris as he turned to walk back to the lounge while reading the note. "Well," Chris mumbled to no one in particular, with slight disgust in his voice, "it was a nice night for a drive." He took his seat, settled back in his chair and slowly finished his beer. Then, he paid the tab and slowly walked out with both hands thrust deep in his coat pockets, through the lobby, out the big glass door and into the cold northwest wind to his car. "God! But some nights are lonely," he said to himself. It was 8:30.

Ellen had to hurry to get to the Vicksburg by 8:30. At first she thought she had plenty of time, but just as she was leaving the store, one of the new sales girls had caught her and unloaded her troubles on Ellen. Ellen could remember her first days on the job, so she had stayed to counsel the girl. It was part of the job she enjoyed the most, but not tonight. *Must not let Paul interfere with my work*, she thought while rushing to the Vicksburg. *Easier said than done*, she noted. She was looking forward to being with him more than she liked to admit.

The parking lot was full, at least close to the door, so Ellen double-parked her car right in front of the lobby effectively blocking traffic. She looked around. *Nobody's coming. I'll just run in a second and see if Paul left a note.*

She went to the desk and inquired. "Yes we have a message for Ellen Nantucket. The gentleman sends his regrets. He had another appointment." It was said with a slightly sadistic glee. Ellen just realized what it must look like to the desk man. She couldn't help chuckling at his misguided glee. This covered up her disappointment at not being able to see Paul, and she dashed back to her car. As she exited

50

the main door, she noticed her headlights seemed a bit dim. She lifted up her collar for protection from the wind chill, and as she got closer, she could tell the motor wasn't running. "Now what!" she ranted. Once in the car, the relief from the biting wind was welcome. *Back just in time*, she thought, as the headlights from a car pulling up behind her glared from the rearview mirror. She turned the key. Nothing. Tried it again. Nothing. "Why now! Why me! Why! Why! Why!"

She noticed a shadow by her window. She tried to roll it down but it was frozen in place. Opening the door a crack, she looked up. "Won't start," she said, "I don't know what's wrong."

"Did you flood it?"

"No, it won't start—won't even make a noise," replied Ellen.

"Mind if I try?" As he leaned down, Ellen could make him out: male, youngish, husky. Looks trustworthy.

"I – I – I guess so," Ellen said uncertainly, not knowing whether to get out or slide over.

"Slide over," said the man. "Name's Christopher, and we got to get this Mustang out of the traffic pattern."

"Okay," said Ellen, "but it won't start."

The young man slid lightly into the seat, tried to start it and confirmed Ellen's diagnosis. "Won't start, just like you said. Sharp gal! Slide back over and steer ahead, off to the right, up against that curb over there. I can push. It's a little downhill." He got the car pushed to the curb and opened the driver's side door. "What are you going to do now?" he was rubbing his hands together.

"I don't know."

"Look, if you like, I can drive you to the 24-hour station just across the freeway. We can have them tow it in and—move over a bit would

51

you? Let me in out of this wind—thanks—whew, that's better."

"I couldn't—you're busy—I don't know you—why..."

"Let me finish," he interrupted. "They can tow your car over to the garage and fix it. I think it's probably the alternator. Wouldn't take 'em long to fix it. But, being a woman they might try to rip you off. Besides, my friend couldn't make it tonight, so I have nothing better to do than help a damsel in distress."

Silence.

"Well, how about it? A sincere boy scout type offer."

"Okay, okay, I'll pay you for your troubles. I don't need charity," replied Ellen, still not sure, but caught in a bind.

"We'll see about that," quipped Chris. "Now let's get in my car and see if we can get you fixed."

About an hour later, having gotten the car towed and a new alternator ordered to be installed, Chris and Ellen agreed to drive to a nearby pancake house for coffee while waiting for her car to be repaired. "Tell me about yourself, you who calls himself Christopher."

Ellen had found Christopher to be quite delightful and non-threatening. Almost a free spirit...almost.

"It's Chris, by the way. Not really much to tell," responded a more subdued Chris. "I live in St. Paul, work for my father on construction, and pick up pretty girls when their alternators don't work. Oh, my middle name is William. When you know my middle name you know all about me." Chris ended on an upbeat note, determined to enjoy the present – not brood about the past or plan for the future. "Now it's your turn, what are you all about, Cinderella?"

"It's obvious I'm not a mechanic," countered Ellen, "otherwise, well, I work for a chain of dress shops as a buyer and supervisor. I enjoy it quite a lot, too. I think it's important to enjoy your work. Do you enjoy construction work, Chris?" The emphasis was on the *you,* as suddenly the conversation became a little heavier than she intended.

Chris leaned forward in his chair bringing his coffee cup to his lips and looked over the top of Ellen's head to a point about thirty miles away. He then placed both hands around the cup as if to warm them and said, "Hey, it's snowing again. I thought we were done with that for a while."

The small talk continued as Ellen enjoyed the hamburger she ordered once she realized how hungry she was. The hour passed quickly as they talked easily about the past football season of the Minnesota Vikings, and about the Twins' chances for the coming year. Ellen surprised Chris with her knowledge of sports. She had followed Steve's career through high school, and because he was an outstanding athlete, she had naturally become interested in the sports he played, even following them with some enthusiasm after Steve was killed.

"I wonder if they have my car done by now?"

Chris knew the hour was up, yet he wished time would stand still. He never was very comfortable with women, but Ellen was different. He was enjoying her company and didn't want it to end. "Should be done by now. S'pose we should head over and check on it. Let's go." Now that their time had run out, Chris wanted to get it over with.

In the car, Ellen could sense a moodiness about Chris, but she didn't know him well enough to interpret it. Steve used to have his moods, too, she thought, guess we all do to some extent. "Thanks," Ellen said softly, apologetically, "for taking the time and trouble to help out a stranger. Really, thanks!"

"What do you mean? I know you," Chris said lightly, regaining some buoyancy, "You're Cinderella and I'm—I'm Chris contractor, the caped crusader." They both laughed, seemingly at Chris' improved mood. "You know what we should do, Cinderella? How long since you've been to a North Stars hockey game?"

"Once last year," replied Ellen, "my one and only time." They pulled into the station and as Chris turned off the car, he turned to Ellen, put his right arm across the top of the seat and let his fingers touch her shoulder, as if to hold her in place.

"What do you say we take in a game, you and me?"

"I don't know," stammered Ellen, "I mean..."

"Look, the North Stars play Chicago here one week from tonight. I'll get a couple tickets, and we'll call it our one week anniversary. What do you say?"

Ellen was watching Chris' eyes. They were almost pleading, though his voice was casual. *I guess I owe him*, thought Ellen, *and he really is a nice sort*. "Sounds good, Chris, let's do it. My number is in the phone book. Ellen Nantucket. The only one there."

"Great! I'll call you in the next couple days."

"I hope my car is done. Would you care to accompany me into the station while I settle up? After all, I wouldn't want to get ripped off," she laughed.

Heading for home through the light snowfall, Ellen wondered about this new turn in her life. At her age and at her discretion, there was no such thing as a truly casual date. Each date, each time out brought her closer to a possible commitment. Maybe she was getting more desperate, maybe more tired, maybe frustrated, maybe unfulfilled. Now with two men to consider having a future with, it should make her feel more secure. It didn't.

"Steve, oh Steve, will I ever find a man as good as you?" Ellen softly repeated. She didn't bother to wipe away the single tear that trailed across her rosy cheek.

6

FEBRUARY 1973
NORTH STARS

"Paul, I thought you were going to miss another meeting." This was the greeting Paul received from Chris as he approached the booth in a northeast Minneapolis bar. Two days had passed since their failed meeting and Chris' chance meeting with Ellen. Paul glanced around as he slid smoothly into the seat across from Chris.

"Sorry about missing it," replied Paul. "I told you what might happen, and it did."

"No problem," said Chris. "In fact, it may have been my lucky day!"

"Well, I'm glad you're not upset then. Anyway, let's get down to business." Paul's face was tipped down, but he looked across at Chris with his forehead wrinkled and his eyes steady. It was a look that invited Chris to begin if he had anything to add. He didn't.

"The new client I met two nights ago was just the situation I've been dreaming about. He represents a bank group. He wants us to design three prototype banks: one for smaller communities, one a little bigger, and one for medium-sized locations. We're supposed to find three contractors who will bid the jobs, then have them keep their bids up-to-date every three months. Anytime they want to put up one of those banks they'll know the cost without the usual time lag of drawing up plans and getting bids. They'd like us to make sure that from the time they announce a new location until the first customer walks in, it's no longer than 120 days. Whenever they do something, they want to move fast to give the impression in any given community that they can make things happen. It's a new concept for them, and us, and it's tailor-made for our plans, almost like a divine stroke of luck!"

"You mean all these banks are going to look the same, like a chain of hamburger stores?" quizzed Chris. "I thought banks were very concerned about maintaining the individual look tailored to the community. Times are changing," he balked.

"Not exactly," replied Paul. "Part of the job is to design cosmetic alternatives so no two banks look exactly the same, but any design within the size limitations must be able to be built for the agreed upon price. I've got to make a preliminary presentation in 30 days, and if our firm gets the job, it'll be nine months later that our designs are supposed to be ready. Chris, we're going to get the job and your company is going to just happen to get the inside track on the construction of the banks. Man! We couldn't have asked for a better deal."

"My job is cut out for me then," said Chris, half to himself and half to Paul. "I'll have to learn more about construction than I know now. I'll have to find a trusted super who'll work for me instead of my dad. We'll need more up-to-date equipment, so that we can get in and get out."

"Don't forget to cultivate some sub-contractors while you're at it," said Paul. "Once we show we can get the job done on time, money won't be a big problem. We'll work a deal so the subs can get a little bonus if they perform well. They'll *want* to work for you."

"You know, it's a good thing we're patient. This thing is going to drag out for several years. I wonder if it wouldn't be easier to plant a bomb somewhere. We could do that on a weekend." Chris ended with a sly grin, then put his hand out with palm extended towards Paul. "I know, I know. Don't say a word. We must be patient, plan well, and carry out the plan well. We'll take the money and use it to affect changes as we see fit at that time. Right? Right! Don't worry, I'm with you one hundred percent."

"Great, great," replied Paul. "Look, don't buy any new equipment or do anything drastic till we land the job for sure. It's not in the bag yet. But, I'm really going after this job, and I'll get it!" Paul was sliding out of the booth. "I'll call you in about a month unless something comes up. Here's a five. Pick up my tab – thanks, and take care."

Chris watched Paul turn the corner and vanish into a crowd at the door. Glancing at his watch he noted it was 6:00 and dark outside. He had gotten two tickets to next week's North Stars game, but hadn't yet called Ellen. Confusion? Fright? Neither? *Why is it so hard to call her? She did say I could.*

Paul is okay, Chris was switching thoughts back to their major upcoming project, but *Paul had always been conservative, unlike me. But, maybe that is a good thing. As for me, I always like the big move. Take a chance: win big or lose big.*

Chris fondled his half-empty beer glass, oblivious to the noise around him. *Who caused this lousy war? Who was responsible for even now making him spend his time in this manner? Politicians, that's who!* His dad had said many times that they were all a bunch of crooks: congressmen, the President and his cronies, the whole lot. *The best thing that could happen is if they had to pay the same price my absent buddies had to pay. It would only be right. An eye for an eye. Each bank we clean out ought to be enough to hire a hit man to take care of one, maybe two of those men responsible for the deaths of all the Jess'*

58

and Bill's in the war. Vindication for the fatherless children, the husbandless wives, the childless parents. Chris' mind raced on. *They ride around in their big cars, go home to their comfortable houses and families like nothing has happened—not even an 'I'm sorry.' By God, I'll take my time, work with Paul if it takes ten years. They'll pay. If Paul won't go along with me, I'll do it myself.* A sense of real purpose solidified. Now real meaning connected with accomplishing this plan, no matter what it would take. *We're still at war in Nam, I'm still at war, here.* With that thought he brought his beer glass down to the table with a sharp blow, hitting it just a bit too hard. The glass broke, creating plenty of noise. He looked around and noticed the bartender coming over.

"Here's for the glass and beer." Chris added a ten to the five Paul had left and handed it to the bartender as he slid out of the booth and headed for the door. His way was blocked by a fairly large guy, probably the bouncer, who glanced at the bartender. The bartender shook him off, so Chris was free to go. Looking down he saw his hand was bleeding from a nasty cut. Wrapping his handkerchief around it slowed the bleeding. "Damn!"

"Might as well," Chris said out loud as he spotted a phone booth at the end of the block.

Ellen almost hoped Chris wouldn't call, and when a few days went by, she had mostly forgotten about him. He had not forgotten, however, and called her to set a plan. It was with mixed feelings she agreed to meet him at the Met Center. He had offered to come by and pick her up at her apartment, but she had made up a story about having to stop at one of the dress shops first. He was easily persuaded. She didn't want this to seem like more of a date than it was. *Something's different about*

Chris, she thought. *He has negative vibes, yet I'm attracted to him in a strange way, like we have stuff in common. Maybe it's nothing,* thought Ellen, as she backed her Mustang out of the driveway and headed to the hockey game. *Maybe I'm overreacting and trying to make something out of nothing,* she thought, as she headed to the hockey game.

The evening was cold and crisp, typical for this time of year, yet invigorating. Certainly conducive to a hockey game, were hot coffee and fireplaces. "Where would you like to go for refreshments, Cinderella?" Chris and Ellen were jostling through the crowd after the game's final buzzer.

"Uh, you can call me Ellen. The Pimento is just down the beltway. We could meet there and have a nightcap, I guess."

"You know what, Ellen just doesn't cut it for me. How about Ellie?"

"That's fine. I had some friends in school call me that. I'm taking my car. I'll meet you in a few minutes."

The hockey game had been exciting and they both had gotten caught up in it. Chris was relaxed after Ellen had agreed to come to the game. It had been especially fun for him because she knew the game's rules and strategy, making it easy to comment on and follow the game together. Chris wanted to drive them both over to the Pimento and then back to the parking lot, but Ellen had insisted on driving herself. She noticed Chris was quite moody after that exchange. She almost felt like she owed him more company, or time, or something. *He is a good sort,* she thought. *I don't know what is holding me back.* Yet, there was a feeling.

She remembered how she had become more sensitive to her own inner feelings after coming back from Japan. After her choir tour ended, she had made arrangements to stay there. Steve had a two-week leave coming up, so they spent that time together. It was glorious. Among other things, they took a quickie course in kung fu. She liked the outer physical training, but enjoyed the inner mind training even more.

After Steve went back to Vietnam, she returned home. Shortly after that she was notified of Steve's death. It was horrible. After a week off work, she tried to go back but couldn't do it. Mrs. Thoms had an idea. She had a sister in New York who worked with her before she hired Ellen. Her sister could come back and help out at the store until Ellen was done grieving.

Ellen arranged to go back to Japan for another five and a half months, engaging in counseling with a well-recommended expert and continued her kung fu training. She also did some song writing and worked part time in a dress shop that specialized in American clothes for Americans living in Japan, though most of their business, surprisingly, was Japanese.

Through a Japanese man she met there, she continued to develop in the physical and mental arts traditional to the Far East. Five and a half months was not a long time for gaining expertise, but she was very athletic and dedicated, so she improved quite fast. After her mental and physical development in this discipline, she felt ready to go on, emotionally, with life.

Anyway, the vibes are not quite right, she thought, as she finished her drink while turning down Chris' offer of another. "Got to be going," she reported to Chris, hoping the speed of her leaving would surprise him before he could get up enough nerve to ask her out again. "Chris, thanks for the nice time," Ellen tried to sound matter-of-fact friendly, not friendly-friendly. As she rose to leave, Chris grabbed her by the arm in a firm but non-threatening way.

"Ellie, I'm just back from Nam—Vietnam. I don't know if you know anybody who's been there but—well, sit down would you?"

Ellen looked around as if seeking an escape route, then glancing at Chris, reseated herself heavily. *Vietnam! Do I know anybody? Jesus yes! Do I*, she thought. Her eyes misted up as she reached in her purse for a Kleenex. Knock it off! She said to herself. Chris needs somebody to talk to.

"Go ahead, Chris, I'm just getting a cold," she fibbed as she dabbed at her nose.

Chris' hand kept a gentle pressure on her forearm, which continued as he pulled his chair closer to hers. "Everything gets turned around for me, and sometimes I don't know what to do. One night I dream of the faces of those I killed in our raids, not knowing if they were the real enemy or just some innocent village people who got in the way. The next night I dream of being captured by the VC, that is the Viet Cong, and tortured in ways you would not want to hear about. You can't imagine the stories the escaped prisoners come back with."

Ellie closed her eyes and squeezed them tightly together as she put her hand over Chris' hand on her arm. She gave it an involuntary squeeze. Chris did not seem to notice as he continued on, almost in a trance. *I sure hope that...that Steve didn't suffer those atrocities at the hand of the Viet Cong*, thought Ellen. The Air Force had given her no information concerning Steve's death. *He probably died immediately upon impact as his plane crashed*, she had chosen to believe.

Chris finished, apparently, as his eyes seemed to return to the here and now. "Maybe you don't want to hear this kind of stuff, Ellie, but I have to tell someone. And, I'll tell you another thing. This war is not over. They're still fighting there, and there will be some fighting here.

Whole bunch of people got some debts to pay. Hey, I know you don't really understand unless you've been there, but me and a whole lot of vets still fight this damn war every day."

"Yes," Ellen replied softly, settling back in her chair. "I bet it was rough," her thoughts racing a hundred miles an hour.

"*Was* rough?" Chris said disgustedly, "*Is* rough! Every time I hear a loud or sharp noise my heartbeat triples and I just catch myself before diving to the ground, and around a construction site it happens a hundred times a day. You know, how important can day-to-day work be any more when you've dealt out death? When you've actually pulled a trigger and killed somebody. I mean, another human being – a flesh and blood person! A man with a wife and three children. Some mother's son or some daughter's father, some sister's brother. Somebody—Jesus! Another person who had the same fears, hopes, emotions, and dreams you did, and then—bang! He's gone. Dead. Then you do it again, and again, and again! What's left in life? I mean, really, laying a few bricks, moving a little dirt, fixing somebody's car, selling dresses—what does it really matter?"

Chris paused, placed both hands around his drink on the table, looked at Ellen, who was speechless, glanced at the ceiling, then back to Ellen, and said softly, emotions in check, "Ellie, tell me it matters. Make me believe it."

Driving home, Ellen wondered what she could have done. Even now the options were not clear. *He needs so much more help than I can give.* She had agreed to be called again. After all, she could contribute a little to this war. Steve had contributed everything. She could certainly counsel with Chris. It was better than doing nothing. She did suggest he avail himself to military counseling, which he probably would not do.

He apparently had nobody he could really talk to, but desperately needed help.

Maybe I could have told him about Steve, she thought. But, no. Chris needed to talk tonight, not listen to her sad story. She was worried about him.

7

FEBRUARY 28, 1973
HARLOW

Matt was away from the main job site, so Chris drove a little out of his way to check in with him at the other location before heading to the site. He needed to find out if there was anything the workers needed his help with while Matt was away for the day. "Mornin', Pops. Need me to check on anything at the main site today?"

"No, Son, I have my man, Rusty, in charge over there today. He's not the sharpest pencil in the box, but he can handle today's work. The men like him. They call him Trusty Rusty, so he must be okay. Anyways, you can go over and check with him if you want."

Chris ran a couple errands on the way over, and arrived at the site at about 11:00 a.m. Trusty Rusty seemed to have everything under control. He headed straight for the construction shack. As he swung the door open, he heard a shriek. "Oh, it's you," sighed Harlow. "I wasn't expecting anyone. I'm checking the time cards, as usual."

"Okay, yah, I've been getting my check on time so it's all good." This was the second time Chris happened to be in the shack when she was there. "Are you a CPA, or what's the deal?"

"Yes, another lady—a CPA also—and I have a small accounting firm. We have five bookkeepers working for us now. We have quite a bit of business from other small businesses like this." She sat back and put her hands behind her head. "What's your story?" she asked, as she gave him an appraising look. She noticed a well-built confident young man, and fairly friendly it seemed.

Chris gave her an abbreviated bio, while she looked him in the eye and nodded as he included his Vietnam tour of duty.

"How long you been back?" He filled her in. "You got yourself a girlfriend then?" she asked.

"Well, not really. But, there's still time. I do have a prospect, though," he laughed. "We'll see how that works out."

"Don't wait too long," she replied, "or you'll be stuck with an old lady like me."

He laughed, "I could do a lot worse." He gave her an appraising look at the same time. She gave him a warm smile and got back to work. Chris was looking at the plans for a small commercial remodel he was going to tackle more or less on his own. His pencil rolled off the desk, while Harlow was nearby at an open file cabinet. As he bent down to locate his lost pencil, he backed into Harlow, butt to butt.

"Whoa!" she said. "You did that on purpose, didn't you?" as she gave a low chuckle.

"Not really, but I should take credit for being sneaky like that."

"Want to try that again?" she said, giving him that warm smile that was beginning to grow on him.

"If I didn't know better, I would think you are trying to start something," Chris said with a nervous laugh. He noticed she wore a wedding ring, so was a little confused as to what was happening. His first date in a long time had been Ellie, and he already liked her a lot, but this could be something different. He was nervous around women, but Harlow seemed approachable. *Why not*, he mused to himself.

"You know what, Harlow?" He looked around to see if anybody might be heading to the shack, "I'd like to get you in a room alone and see who blinks first."

She sat back down in her chair, looked him in the eye, drew a pencil across her lips and said, "Yah, we could try that."

"Let's go," he said, "I don't have to be here."

"Give me five minutes to finish checking these cards, we can stop at the Holiday Inn about three blocks from my office. You go get checked in while I wait in my car, bring me a key and room number, then I'll run these time cards to my office so the girls can start on them, and I'll be back."

"Doesn't sound like you're doing any blinking—yet."

After he followed her to the motel and had delivered her the key, he headed back to the room. "Wow," he muttered to himself, "what am I getting into?" He took a shower and was just putting his last shoe on when the door opened and Harlow came in.

"Well, now what?" she sighed, as she slipped out of her winter coat.

"Sit on this recliner," Chris said nervously, "and relax. You want some coffee from the little coffee maker over there?"

"You having some?" she asked.

"I've got it heating up now, so I'll make two cups." He gave her a cup and sat on the edge of the bed. "You nervous?" he said.

"More than I thought I would be."

"Me too. Maybe this will help." He went around behind her and ran his fingers through her hair. "I like your hair," he remarked, as he moved under her hair and started to massage her shoulders and neck. "How does that feel?"

She closed her eyes and sat forward a little. "Oh my god," she murmured. "That feels great." He continued for several minutes as she made sounds of contentment. He massaged the top of her arms, which she kept close to her body so he couldn't help but feel the sides of her breasts with the back of his hands. No blinking. He massaged back up to her neck and reached around front to her cheeks and mouth. He drew his finger across her lips and she painted it with her tongue. He gently grabbed a handful of hair and pulled her head back so he could look into her eyes.

"You okay?" he said, as he massaged her cheeks lightly.

"More than okay," she replied dreamily. He let go of her hair and massaged down the front of her until he could feel the swell of her breasts, then he trailed off to each side and down to her hips. He bent over and kissed her right below her right earlobe, then did the same on the left. Then he tongued each ear unhurriedly. He could feel her shiver. He started massaging at the neck again, down to the same point where he lifted his hands and barely skimmed her sweater, over her breasts, then down her stomach to the belt on her jeans. He started again, this time with a little more pressure, and when he got to the jeans, he unhooked her belt, with no resistance. On the way back up he grasped the bottom of her sweater and pulled it up. She lifted her arms in the air so he could complete the maneuver. She had on a black lacy bra that made him smile in anticipation.

Looks like I got myself to the point of no return, thought Harlow. She had tried dating a couple times in the last two or three years, but no one even got to first base. The guys were way too much into themselves, grabby, and after just one thing. Or, so it seemed to her. Besides, it felt like cheating. But, Chris seemed different. *Why not give it a go*, she thought.

He took off his shirt, went around to the front of her chair and pulled her up where he held her at arms' length as he appraised her. Then he took her face gently in his hands, told her to close her eyes and not do anything. He pulled her face to his and he let his lips lightly touch hers, he held that for several seconds, then he traced the outline of her lips with his tongue. She tried to reciprocate, but he told her to wait. He pulled her tight, she put her arms around him as their lips locked and tongues fought. After a couple minutes he pushed her back while holding her arms. "If you're going to blink, you better do it now or it may be too late."

"Same to you cowboy," she said as she walked back into his arms.

Later, after an encore, Harlow said she had to go. There were just some things she had to get done today. He offered to take her to dinner, but she took a rain check. "Too close to the office, too close to home. Uh, will you be at the office a week from now?"

"Count on it," he said.

"Funny meeting you here," Harlow said as she entered the construction shack a week later. She looked around quickly and out the dirty curtain to ascertain they were alone.

"I heard you were in town so I thought I would see if there was anything you needed." Chris joked. He had eagerly waited for this day to arrive and had hoped that Harlow would show. Apparently, she was fine with the last meeting, because here she was. Of course, her arrival could be to tell him to drop dead, too.

"Well, do you want to watch the same movie again?"

"I really loved it, can't get enough of it." Chris replied. "There is a Rodeway Inn about a block from that Holiday Inn. Maybe we shouldn't hit the same place twice."

"Good idea. It'll take me half an hour to check these time cards, so busy yourself and we'll get out of here." She sat down in Matt's chair and started working. Chris couldn't help himself, so he snuck around behind her, wrapped her up and kissed her neck and ears. As he started to run his hands down her front, "Get out of here!" she said mockingly. "I'll never get anything done with you breathing down my neck." She shooed him away. He knew she was right. The sooner she got done, the sooner they could go.

"You know what? I should leave *now*. If someone sees that we always leave together, someone will put two and two together. I have a couple errands to run, then I'll wait for you in front of the Rodeway Inn. You know the one?" She nodded. "45 minutes?" She nodded. "Don't be late." He laughed as he left.

They had met, he gave her the key and room number, and she was on the way to drop off paperwork at her office. As he sat on the bed getting dressed after his shower, he wondered if this is what he really wanted. He came to the conclusion, that, for now, it was. Ellie...I could really fall in love with her, but she doesn't seem all that much into me. Not as a boyfriend, anyway. I get no feeling that she and I will get to this stage for a long, long time. She will come around. I know it. But this is good – for now.

The door swung open and Harlow came in, threw her coat on the chair, grabbed Chris and pulled him close. Their kissing became frantic and soon she was working his clothes off him and he was doing the same to her. This time they had no time for preliminaries and got to the main event right away.

"Wait," she said later, "don't go. Lay on top of me longer. Just lay and hold me for a while. Quietly." He had no problem with that. After a while he could tell he was getting a bit heavy, so he slid off.

She excused herself, and soon he heard the shower. She came out toweling off, but made no move to put anything on. He had purposely turned the heat up when she was showering, hoping it would have this effect. She came over by the bed where he was still laying, naked as a jaybird. He noticed how toned she was. "I've got a couple questions, if you don't mind. If you do, just tell me to mind my own business." She sat down on the side of the bed so she could make eye contact, as he was laying back on a pillow with his arms over his head.

"What is it?" she asked.

"You look in great shape, especially for an older woman, er—and I mean that in the best possible way," he quickly added.

She chuckled, "I work at it. I have a regimen I follow every day, watch my diet, and belong to the Northwest Biathlete club. You know what that is?"

"Yah, sure," said Chris, "I watch the Olympics. The biathlon is shooting and skiing, right?"

"Right. But, we also do running and shooting when we can't ski. I actually got an Olympic tryout several years ago. Had an off day, but the other women were very good."

"And," Chris said, then hesitated.

"What is it? Go ahead. Wait, I know what you want to know," continued Harlow. "What about my wedding ring, right?"

"Yesss, but it's none of my business—I think."

"I'll tell you. Stop me if you heard it before. I was madly in love with an older man when I was 17. He was off to the Korean War, and I wanted to marry him after basic training. My folks wouldn't let me. As soon as I turned 18 and he came home on leave, in 1952, we got married. It was my lifelong dream to find my soulmate, and we had the most glorious week of marriage anybody could ever want." Harlow finished drying her hair and had crawled back in bed next to Chris under a light blanket, as it seemed cooler now. "Of course he had to go back to Korea. They were still fighting the war. It finally ended, and he was coming home. I could hardly wait. Each day of waiting seemed like an eternity. On the day he left Korea for home he had a low fever. But, on the way home it got worse and worse. When he got to Minneapolis, I took him right to the Veteran's hospital. Unfortunately his paperwork had not caught up with him. Even in his uniform, they could not admit him until the paperwork showed. We sat there all day, into the night. I still remember like it was yesterday, though it's been about 20 years now. He had a convulsion in the waiting room, so they finally found him a bed." She paused, and he could see her eyes were swelling with tears. "But, but, it was too late. He's still in the Veteran's home, but doesn't know anything—not even me." She barely got that out, threw back the cover and ran to the bathroom.

When she came out she was dressed as was he. He took her hand and beckoned her to sit on the edge of the bed. "My God, Harlow. I am so sorry. It makes me so mad that the VA allowed that to happen. But, I am not surprised. How do you feel about it now?"

"If I could find the people responsible, I would kill them. They cost me my soulmate and any children we may have had, and the happiness that a family like that brings. I know I could have divorced him and married again, but I'll never leave him, never! I think, under the circumstances, he would approve of you and me, but I guess this is as good a time as any. This, what we have, whatever it is, will never go anywhere. I just think you should know that. Okay?"

"I understand. Look, why don't we grab an early dinner someplace away from your usual haunts? I'd like to talk to you some more about this."

"Okay, I'm too wrung out to do anything anyway. I'll ride with you and you can swing by here after, so I can get my car. Will that work?"

Chris knew of a decent nightclub that would suit their needs. After ordering their food, their drinks arrived. They were pretty much by themselves, as it was too early for the nightlife crowds. "Harlow, have you ever thought of getting even for what happened to you. I mean, did you write letters, call anybody, do any follow up?"

"I wrote to my Senator and Representative. Both sent letters from their aides; form letters. How insulting. I wrote the VA and heard nothing. I was helpless. Remember, I was all of 19 years old at that time. My Pastor helped me get to a place in my mind where it is best to move on. But you see, I still have my wedding ring on. I really haven't moved on, and now it's getting worse. I feel more and more bitter and just as helpless. I'm afraid it might affect my business. I just feel I should do something. Make something happen, but I don't know what."

"Let me ask you," said Chris, "*who* are you bitter at?"

"First of all, in hindsight, what did we accomplish in Korea that was worth 30,000 young men killed in action and over 100,000 wounded? Every one of those people had a mother and father. Many had wives and children whose lives were turned upside down, like mine. And, even the hundreds of thousands of our troops that escaped physical damage did not escape psychological damage. You can't blame the troops, or even the generals. They were doing what they were told to do. The President did this, and Congress did nothing to stop it. As always, with wars, a bunch of old men sending a bunch of young men to fight their war. Geez, I got to stop this!" With that she sat back, exhausted, and let out a distressed sigh.

"Yes, it's hard, feeling betrayed and helpless. Harlow, how far would you go to try to make things right?"

"As far as I could." She paused and looked right at him. "Does that scare you?"

"Even after 20 years?"

"Even more after 20 years – it's building up."

"I can help. I feel the same way. I lost some good buddies in Nam, which was just as worthless a war as Korea, maybe more so. I'm going to tell you my plan, but you've got to stop me if I start talking about things you don't want to hear about, and you've got to promise me to tell *no one* what I am about to tell you. I am taking a huge chance on you. Okay?"

"Tell me more."

Chris told her, in general terms—no names, no location—of his plans for Congressman Cuppen in New Mexico. Then he asked, "Do you want to come along? Take your time, this is very serious."

She sat for several minutes staring over his shoulder, a thousand miles away. *This is it*, she reflected. *Time to put up or shut up. I've been telling myself I would do whatever I could to get even. Now is my chance. I'm only living half a life anyway. It might as well be all or nothing. There could be some nasty consequences, but if our actions make the next politicians think a little harder before sending our young men off to war, that could be my contribution.* She said, "I'm willing to go with you to see if I can 'stomach' the kind of action you're planning. Just tell me where and when. But, if I want out after the first one, you have to let me go. I will keep my mouth shut. By being at the execution, I am as guilty as you, plus I approve of your actions. It is good to be

74

doing something."

Chris thought she seemed very eager to actually do something instead of just think about it. *That's good. She can help. Especially since she knows her way around a rifle.* "Okay, I'm not going to tell you any more in case you still want to change your mind, but the first action is several months off. This process is going to take patience. I'll give you plenty of warning."

They headed back to the Rodeway Inn to retrieve Harlow's car. As Chris pulled in beside her car, she said, "Chris, I am so beat. We have the room yet, right?" He nodded. "Would you give me a neck massage? That would feel so good."

"Yep, I have the key right here. Inside he turned the heat up. She sat in a chair and he started to massage her neck. After a few minutes, he helped her off with her sweater so he could do a better massage. After a few more minutes, he helped her out of her bra. After a few more minutes neither one had any clothes on, and they laid down and made slow, lazy, delicious love, feeling more connected than ever.

8

The room looked larger than it was, as most empty rooms do. Just a dusty, musty one-room office leased to a fictitious "J. F. Andersen Co." by mail, over three months ago. Cash in advance. Nobody even wondered why it had remained vacant; vacant until now. The occupant had brought up two old, but sturdy, straight-backed chairs purchased from a secondhand store over 100 miles away. There wouldn't be anything left of them after the blast, but one cannot be too careful on one's first murder. Technically, it wasn't his first murder – there had been quite a number in Nam. But, that was not illegal. The U. S. Government had said it was okay to go 8,000 miles away to somebody else's country and murder the locals if they looked suspicious.

Chris carefully let himself and Harlow in the dark, drab room, and after checking the second floor hallway to see if they had been observed, closed and locked the door behind them. He was sure they were alone in the old building, but still he was alert. The musty, wet wallpaper smell reminded him of the basement in his childhood house where he and his mother would hide to escape the tirades of a less-than-sober father and husband.

Harlow had accompanied him. She had convinced Chris she was "all in." They met weekly, and Chris had grown to trust her. So, a week before this trip he explained what was going on and how she would fit in. He had made these plans as a one-person operation. She could

76

accompany him this one time. Until he needed two people for a job, she would remain behind after this initial *test*. Until then, he was not going to risk his original plans, not for anything – or anyone. She was okay with that, for now. She could help with supplies and other planning, and eventually they would execute one of *her* plans. But, not just yet.

The brown, pebbly suitcase was placed on the floor, unlocked, and then opened. Chris caressed the wood grain stock before slowly and deliberately removing the death instrument from its appointed place. The scope was professionally attached into its pre-drilled, pre-fitted holes.

A Swiss "Bearluger" was a precision weapon. It was a shame to waste it, and it didn't come cheap. It cost him plenty at a gun show in Reno. Next, a small handsaw was removed, and Chris cut the legs of each chair so that it was exactly 28 inches to the top of the chair back. Two stainless steel clamps were applied and the Bearluger was placed in the clamps.

A drop of sweat fell on the creamy wood stock as Chris lined the rifle up with the window. The shade was still pulled even though it was almost impossible to see into the single, dirty window that attempted to brighten this dreary office. Chris cut a small hole in the shade so that, when he looked through the scope and the hole, he could see the speaker's stand set up at street level outside. The new, metal folding chairs reflected the hot noonday sun. He let Harlow take a look. She nodded in approval. A glance at his watch showed it to be 12:30 p.m. *One hour to go,* mused Chris. *One hour before the illustrious Congressman David C. Cuppen, of Santa Fe New Mexico, dedicates his latest and last pork barrel project.*

Chris knew that David C. Cuppen could talk and talk and talk, when given the chance – just as he had at the beginning of the Vietnam "police action." He was one of the loudest supporters of military action and one of the first and loudest to restrict real efforts at *winning* the "war." They insisted, as Chris used to say, on making us fight with one hand tied behind our back.

Well, a thousand David C. Cuppens aren't worth one of my Nam buddies, thought Chris. *No doubt in my mind. I'll make sure he and some of his friends won't get a chance to make the same mistake again. They will pay.*

The chairs were firmly screwed in place, a plunger properly fastened on one, the Swiss killing stick on the other, aimed directly one foot behind the speaker's podium and securely clamped in place. The electrical timing device was set for precisely 1:45 p.m. At that time, it would activate the plunger which would smoothly, without jerking, pull the trigger back. The gun would fire and the heavy plunger would continue its rearward movement, tipping the chair and collapsing it on a small amount of plastic explosive just as that timer also activated the explosive.

The chairs, the gun, fingerprints, and the shabby building would mostly end up a pile of rubble – so would the life of Congressman Cuppen. It had worked in practice, minus the explosives, ten times without fail. Chris had no reason to believe it wouldn't work today, the eleventh.

Boarding time for flight 186 from Santa Fe to Denver to Minneapolis was 1:40 p.m., and "Donald Larson" and "Amanda Wright" were on time. Waiting for take-off, Chris wondered if the television had flashed the breaking news yet. *Patience...* he'd just have to settle down and wait

78

until they stopped in Denver for the two-hour layover. Once airborne, it was always easier to relax. *There's just something about your life being completely out of your hands, or something like that*, thought Chris. He took Harlow's hand and smiled a weak smile as she looked at him. There wasn't much to say.

I wonder why Paul can't see my point of view, Chris thought, as he replayed his last meeting with Paul. *He wants to move so slowly and deliberately. We'd never get anywhere.* Chris had argued that point ten ways to Sunday. Chris never fully revealed what he was going to do, not even close, only that they should do *something* sooner rather than later. And, he was never going to tell Paul about Harlow and their assassination plans either, or vice versa. "We've only just got our first AmBank to design. It'll take some time," Paul had said. Chris could still hear it like an echo – *take some time...take some time*. Well, he was going to *take some lives* and get some payback for Jess and Bill, and all the others. They had waited long enough. He had waited long enough.

9

AUGUST 20, 1973
VETERAN'S HOSPITAL

In the six months he had been at Vicksburg Veteran's Hospital, Sergeant James (Jim) E. Tonger had not said a word, had not taken one step, or acknowledged pain, heat, or cold…or any person for that matter. He was a classic cataleptic. There was no physical reason keeping him from being awake, responsive and normal; normal as a person could be with spine damage that apparently would keep him from using his legs ever again. He arrived back in the US as part of the prisoner exchange of medical patients in March of 1973 in this condition. Despite the best attempts at the hospital, he had not changed one iota since. That's why RN Sara Forsyth was so excited on August 6th, 1973. On her evening rounds she saw tears dribbling down the cheeks of the patient in Room 306 – the first sign of any reaction to the outside world at all, by Sergeant Tonger. She checked him closely. Just tears, no other reaction. No acknowledgement of any stimulus, yet.

Dr. Rod McKenny had too much to do to be sitting at his desk. Leaning back in his antique leather office chair and looking over his steepled hands, he wondered what horrible tragedy had happened to Sergeant James E. Tonger to make him escape from life and what inexplicable force had brought him back. Oh, he wasn't back yet, not by a long way. But now, two weeks after Sara had discovered the tears, Sergeant Tonger was making slow, gradual progress towards reality. He had seen this 'miracle' happen a few times before, just a very few. The patient still had very serious spinal damage, probably from a steel pipe across the back. Who knows what happened in Vietnam prisoner camps. He had seen some bad results and heard some terrible stories. But, at least for Sergeant Tonger, the journey back had finally started.

"Sara!" Dr. McKenny had just caught sight of the very attractive looking brunette as she walked by his office door. *Five foot two, eyes of blue*, always crossed his mind when he saw her, only she was 5'-6" with eyes of blue. About 24, sparkly, smart, slightly cool, but friendly, she was the perfect professional…almost.

"Yes, Dr. McKenny," she leaned back into the doorway opening looking at the slightly graying, distinguished-looking doctor. The mostly white beard was set off by mostly black wavy hair and a rugged tan face. She knew he was tan in a lot more places than showed. She had fallen for him three years ago when she started at the VA. He had not paid any attention to her then, but fell easily after his wife had suddenly succumbed to cancer. Now they saw each other frequently and spent most of their free weekends together at his ocean-side villa.

At the hospital, theirs was a strictly professional relationship. Dr. McKenny stood up and unfolded his 6'-4" lanky frame. "Sara, what are your observations of Sergeant Tonger?"

"It's just gratifying to see him react to light and sound. He can also curl his toes. I think he's going to wake up and be a person. In fact, I'm going to see to it personally."

"Good. I know you've been spending a little of your extra time with him. Tell you what, let's you and I together see that this one makes it!"

"You bet!" She replied enthusiastically. Then she continued down the hall to see Sergeant Jim Tonger. She was glad to have Dr. McKenny encourage her. At times she felt like he was a bit jealous of the time she spent at Jim's bedside. *Maybe that's just my imagination*, she thought. After all, Sergeant Tonger couldn't even talk, walk or communicate in any way. Yet, there was something special about him. Like he *had to* wake up. Like there were things to be done. Whenever she and Rod were alone at his villa and she wanted to talk about Sergeant Tonger, he would cool, noticeably, and change the subject, or not talk at all. Interestingly, they could talk about other cases without any odd reactions. Well, she was a quick learner, so while at the villa she didn't bring up Jim's case anymore.

Sitting in the chair next to Jim's bed, as she had most every day at the end of her 7-3 shift, she took a book from his bedside stand. Opening up to Monday, August 20, 1973, she filled in the day's happenings in the five-year diary she bought for Jim. Looking back through the pages, it reminded her that until two weeks ago, she could only enter what people had done *for* Jim: shaves, haircuts, daily muscle massages, etc. But, starting on August 6th, she could include things that Jim had done. First the tears, then the eyes not yet open, but what seemed to her as some sort of blinking signal when she asked him yes or no questions, and then the hand squeezing. *All signs of progress. Of course, there are a million miles to go*, she thought, as she closed the book and slipped it back in the drawer.

"Jim, how are you doing today?" She had his hand in hers and waited for the expectant return squeeze. None came. "Jim, are you awake or just loafing?" she said as she leaned forward, as if she could coax it out of him. "I'm not going to talk to you if you won't say hello!" she scolded. She always talked to him for 15-20 minutes straight just like he could hear her. She'd had a previous patient in a similar condition and did a case study. The patient eventually "woke up" and reported being able to hear his mother for three or four weeks before he could respond. What a morale builder it had been for this patient. Until the familiar, supportive voice, he was ready to give up.

She felt Jim squeeze her hand the usual two times, then a third, then a fourth! "Why, I believe you did that on purpose, making me wait. In fact I think you're getting a good laugh out of it right now!" It did look like he was smiling, but maybe she wanted so badly to believe that she was seeing with her heart and not her eyes. "Well, okay, since you said 'hello' here goes. Today is August 20, 1973. It's Monday, and it's ten after three in the afternoon. We are in a VA hospital in Vicksburg, Virginia. Today is mostly sunny with a high temperature of 82 degrees. You remember, don't you, that your family is quite small. Just your father, Harold Tonger, living in Baltimore where you were born and raised."

Actually that wasn't all good news, as Sara knew. Jim's dad was in a less than sparkling nursing home in downtown Baltimore. He was also completely senile and would probably not recognize his own son should the opportunity ever arise.

"You have been in the hospital for five months and two weeks. Should you feel like moving, it will be difficult because of a back injury. But, if you should snap out of this Rip Van Winkle routine, we could get to work on that and you'd be good as new." She paused, let go of his hand, and sat back in the chair. She tried to be honest in this daily reality orientation, but she couldn't be completely honest about the back injury. There would be time to deal with that when he became conscious. If he knew the whole truth, he might not have the will to come back. It wasn't all bad, but the X-rays did show some apparently

83

irreversible damage. It was difficult to know how much until therapy could begin. Then, too, a lot depended on the patient's mental attitude and will power. Both medical doctors agreed that the best outcome would be to walk with a walker, and at worst he'd be confined to a wheelchair or bedridden. There would be no way to tell until therapy started, and that couldn't start until the patient regained full consciousness. One fact was known: the back injury had no physical impact on the semi-coma he was in.

She took his hand again and resumed her one-way discussion telling about herself and family. Then, it was on to reporting the day's news and ending with a quiet prayer. "Our Father, Who art in heaven, hallowed be Thy name…"

Jim was listening as hard as he could. *If I could just say something so she doesn't stop coming in.* He tried again to speak, to say something. Nothing. He couldn't remember when she first came in. It seemed like she had always been with him. At first he could not understand anything except the warm touch of her soft hands. Then, it finally registered that he was alive and seemingly safe. The repeated kickings, beatings, cold water, hot water, and other tortures had ended. Though he could not move and felt pain every waking moment, it did seem duller. And, it did seem safer to be awake for longer periods of time, though he still couldn't even open his eyes. *Can't do a damn thing, except squeeze.*

Once, he stayed awake even after he heard voices, and the pain did not increase. He felt a release, a new birth. He felt like crying. Now that familiar voice meant warmth and comfort. She seemed knowledgeable of his situation, and he wanted so desperately to communicate. The hand squeezing was okay but not reliable enough. Sometimes his muscles would do what he wanted and sometimes not. He knew after the word *Amen*, the lady would leave. He tried to hold on to her, but there was no strength in his hands. *Wait. I know I can say something. Sara. Yes, that's her name. Sara, wait.* He knew she was gone. She always pulled the curtain and it darkened the room just a little. He tried to force his eyes open, his mouth to speak, but they wouldn't obey. *I will...I will...I will....*

10

SEPTEMBER 8, 1973
EXECUTION

This execution business is more time consuming than I figured, thought Chris. He was sitting in a lounge at O'Hare. Glancing at his watch, he noticed he had a good hour to wait. Four weeks ago, then again two weeks ago, he had been able to observe Congressman Glenn Danfield, 6th District, Illinois, returning from Washington on Mid-Central flight 907, arrival at 9:10 p.m. Friday. He had departed Sunday afternoon, each time, on Mid-Central 406, a 3:57 departure. Harlow was helping with planning, and a careful reading of the *Chicago Tribune* disclosed that he had a dedication in his district this weekend. So, Chris was there too.

While waiting, his thoughts turned to Ellie. He was sure she liked him, but it was getting harder and harder to get together. I'm busy...*she must be real busy at work since she has so many evening meetings. I guess with ten stores to oversee, it would keep a person busy. I like it when we're together. She seems to understand my problems and is always encouraging me. You would think a girl like that would have two or three boyfriends, but she doesn't seem to have any besides me. Harlow is fun and a great partner, but there is no hope of a family with her. Ellie is the one. She'll see that one day, too. I know she will.*

He had finally convinced Ellie to go to a Twins game with him, and they had a good time. She didn't seem to care to go for drinks, so they had gone for coffee after. At that time she mentioned she had located a

86

Vietnam Veteran's support group which met once a month, and she would be glad to accompany him. If he wanted to go, she would mark her calendar ahead of time so she could make it. He normally wouldn't do something like that, but if it was a way he could get an evening out with Ellie, he was all for it. He knew she liked him – he could just tell. A loud announcement broke his concentration, and he became re-involved with his current assignment.

Apparently Congressman Danfield was a creature of habit. And stubborn. Chris recalled how Danfield had sided against Vietnam involvement and was almost openly pro-Viet Cong. That was the kind of politician that gave encouragement to the enemy. He had even accompanied the famous actress, Julie Janeway, to Hanoi.

The congressman had carried his own luggage. On all four occasions it was the same. A plaid softside piece of "luggageAir" and a brown leather "execucarry" briefcase. Both pieces were quite easy to buy. The softside Danfield was checked and the briefcase he carried on.

Chris rose and started for the Mid-Central baggage claim carrying pieces identical to the Congressman's. The softside already had a pink baggage check on it, hidden for now, inside a slightly larger, decoy piece modified so Chris could pull the duplicate out of the decoy without much fuss. The claim number didn't matter, as they were rarely checked and the Congressman was well-known to the staff. One slight modification to each piece was a sack of sand of the approximate correct weight, fastened securely inside, and a silent timing device plugged into some plastic explosive. Synchronized and deadly, the explosive was already activated according to the flight's arrival time. It was timed to explode as the Congressman was driving his 45-minute route home. *Meticulously planned and practiced, this is it.*

The main stress point, Chris knew, was trading suitcases. The softside piece would simply be set by the mouth of the carousel and slipped on with the first arriving pieces. Hopefully, the Congressman's real piece would not be among the first ten or so, though Chris would get a spot right at the mouth, and, if he had to, could slip it into the empty decoy bag.

But, he would have to trade briefcases on the spot. On previous occasions Chris noted that there was somebody always chatting up the Congressman, and Danfield seemed to enjoy the engagement. Consequently, he didn't pay too much immediate attention to his briefcase, which he always set on the floor beside him.

The baggage claim attendant nodded at Chris as he passed through the roped entrance. He was sure his fake mustache, sun glasses and baseball cap would make later identification impossible. As the guard looked away, Chris slid the two bags under the rope from where he had previously placed them. Since there was luggage sitting around from an earlier flight, it was no problem to move them up near the conveyor mouth.

A few of the younger, faster walkers soon arrived, but no Congressman, yet. He shielded the two pieces with his body, not expecting any problem anyway. He made no eye contact with anybody and remained still and silent, drawing no attention. The area filled rapidly. The flight must have been full, like most Friday night flights. One problem. *Where is he?* The Congressman had not shown up. Chris was not absolutely sure he would be on this flight. There was no way to be certain. He had relied on Danfield's apparent habit of using this airline and flight.

Then, from around the hall corner, he saw him coming. He was in an animated discussion with a plump, middle-aged lady. He seemed to want to be rid of her, but she was not to be denied. As he entered the baggage claim area, he said a few words to the guard, who laughed in return. Then after looking around, he staked a claim at the outer edge of the crowd. *Yep, the seasoned traveler.* As the lady continued to wave her arms, he set his briefcase down near his leg, folded his arms, spread his legs, and settled in to wait.

Chris knew he had to work fast. He had to exchange briefcases then get back before the baggage started moving. He hoped the baggage handlers were slow as usual tonight. He headed toward Danfield, taking care the Congressman would not notice him. He was now standing at his right shoulder, just back enough. Waiting. Pretty soon the baggage would be moving. *C'mon. Hurry up.* He set the duplicate briefcase just behind Danfield's, but out of his immediate sight. *Be patient.* Just then the conveyor started up. People crowded in, and somebody kicked over one of the three glasses of water Chris had set near a post, onto the tile floor, off to the left. Danfield and those nearby glanced over to see what had happened. At the same time, Chris knelt down as if to examine his shoes, picked up Danfield's briefcase and slid the impostor in its place. He backed away and moved back into the crowd forming by the mouth of the luggage conveyor belt just as bags started to come through. He slipped the impostor quickly between two larger pieces and saw Danfield recognize it as it made the turn. Danfield grabbed both pieces and headed for his car.

Chris turned and casually followed him, and watched him dump both pieces in the trunk. Chris was parked nearby and followed a couple cars behind as Danfield left the airport. Traffic had been heavy at the airport, but started thinning out as they merged onto the highway. *That's good,* thought Chris as he passed Danfield's large Oldsmobile. *We don't want any civilian casualties, if we can help it.* Staying right with him didn't matter too much, as Chris knew where he was headed. He decided to keep the impending carnage in his rearview mirror and sped up, passing him. He stayed about a half mile ahead of Danfield and was looking at his watch when his eyes were drawn to the rearview mirror by a bright yellow blast, followed by a pretty good-sized *boom*. Shock waves were felt just as the accelerator was depressed.

Police cars and fire trucks raced past him going in the other direction. By the time he turned towards the Twin Cities, the traffic had died down and the wind had picked up. He wanted to call Harlow, but didn't want to leave any trace that he was in the area. *The FBI can probably trace payphone calls. We're not taking that chance.* It was going to be a long 12 hours home. But, a good 12 hours. A light autumn rain started to fall, distorting objects through the windshield. *It may be nature's metaphor*, thought Chris. The score was beginning to even. The good guys had scored a couple points.

11

Ellen had picked a fantastic Saturday for her day off. The golden yellow morning sun streamed through the open curtains painting a halo around the deck furniture. She yawned, stretched, threw off her light blanket, and padded sleepily past Missy, the fierce-looking lion statue guarding her bedroom door. She had planned to go right back to bed, but was now pretty much awake. *It's only 7:00 a.m.,* she noted as she glanced at the clock, *but let's make it a day.* Shuffling back to her bedroom, her eyes were drawn to the lion by the sun's rays hitting Missy's head and mane. . She laughed. *Wonder what Paul would say if he saw this thing?* "Now you be good." She patted the lion's head.

Missy the lion was a gift from Steve. It was a constant reminder of her brother, not that she needed one, but it was special. He bought it for her when they were together in Japan. She had fallen in love with it at a native art show, although it was outrageously expensive and she had no thoughts of really owning it. Without her knowledge, Steve bought it and arranged shipment to her apartment. It was delivered the same day she was notified of his death.

Now, after a satisfying, leisurely breakfast, Ellen was enjoying an invigorating walk. It helped, she found out, to be physically active. Stimulation for the mind and body forced the memories temporarily into the background. She entered Hiawatha Park, a favorite of her and Steve's. It had a clear lake, ducks, a playground, a picnic area, baseball

91

fields, a wooded area, plenty of grass, and a walkway winding through the gently rolling landscape.

The bright and welcome sun was melting away the coolness of the autumn morning. It was time to rest and take off her light jacket. The brisk walk had given her a sense of well-being. She looked down the walkway from her bench just in time to see a young man dressed in his army uniform skipping down the steps of an apartment across the street. He turned and waited for a young lady who was headed for his waiting arms. After a light embrace, they got in their car and took off. Something in her sense of strength and well-being started to shift.

She heard the swings squeaking their rhythmic song at the top of the little hill in the park, and it became too much. She put her head down and brought her feet up on the edge of the bench. Her arms clasped her knees, pulling her legs in tight, and she buried her head between her knees. The jog suit's polyester fabric soaked up her tears. She sobbed heartily for two or three minutes, oblivious to any passersby. She took a deep breath, released her knees, laid her head back and raised her face to the sun. *Let the tears flow*, she thought. They responded by flowing back past her ears into her hair. Yet, she remained, allowing this cleansing action; cleansing her eyes and soul.

After five minutes, she wiped up a little, got up, and walked slowly to a small valley between two hills that was somewhat isolated. The grass was dry, but she spread out her jacket underneath anyway. *Let's have a good think, right here, right now. I don't have to be ashamed of my feelings for Steve. We were close. I guess we were normal until our parents died, but even that alone does not account for our closeness. Adversity brings people closer together, they say. I guess being a close family when our parents were alive, plus also having to fight against being split up to relatives who were only after what little life insurance there was, made us especially close. Now that might be unusual for siblings, but it is not unnatural.*

Ellen rolled over on her stomach, searching the grass for a four leaf clover. *How old was I when Steve and I had so much fun in this park, 16 or 17? I don't know, maybe about a year after mom and dad died.* There hadn't been much to be happy about during that time. "Don't you do it, Steve! If you swing me any higher I'll die, and when I get off I'll kill you!" They were too old to be playing on the swings at that time. But, they did it anyway. Steve coaxed her onto the swing and pushed her higher and higher. The legs of the whole set raised each time she reached the top. Finally, he stopped, then took off running with Ellen in hot pursuit. He was acting very smart until he tripped on a branch, did a couple barrel rolls, and ended up in the lake, ducks quacking and flying every which way. She laughed so hard she couldn't stand up, and oh how her side had ached from laughing. Steve fished his way out and fell in a soggy heap on top of her, laughing just as hard.

"Missy, I'll get even with you." *Missy*...he was the only one who ever called her that. Finally, their laughter stopped and they looked at each other, eyes filled with happy tears.

"Missy," Steve said, reaching behind her, stroking her hair. "Missy, you are very precious to me." She could remember how his blond hair seemed to glow as his head eclipsed the late afternoon sun. "I know you'll have other men love you in a different way than I, but none more. We've been through a lot this year, you and I, and you have made me very proud of you." He removed his hand from her hair and was holding both her hands in his. "I want you to know that you can call me anytime in your life. I'll be there."

He looked down, let go of her hands, and in a lighter tone said, "This is fun—we needed a good laugh." He tweaked her cheek as they got up. "But, enough is enough. I'm soaked! Last one to the car is a turkey." He was leaning just enough so her light push toppled him over as she raced to the car, one step ahead.

"Okay turkey, give me the keys. I got here first, and besides, turkeys can't drive in this state!"

"Okay, you win, only you pay your own fines!"

Ellen slowly came back to the present. Still in memory-mode she thought, *we complimented each other like few people do. He was even supportive when I had my first date*, she recalled. *He even stayed up until I got home. He didn't pry, but I told him all about it anyway, just as he knew I would. He never did violate my trust in him.*

"Hey!" A collie pup surprised her by licking her lower leg. "Scram! Oh…come here, boy, c'mon. It's okay…" The pup obeyed with its tail between its legs. She petted the friendly pup as it stepped all over her. She was reading its collar tag when the owner appeared and apologetically claimed him.

She hopped up and started the walk home. *What about now? I'm lucky to have found Paul. I like him a lot. He treats me as somebody special. He's intelligent, hard-working, good looking and, yeah, fairly well-to-do. Why can't I let myself fall head over heels in love? Maybe it's because I feel I would be betraying Steve. It's almost like I need him to release me from a bond. Weird. Well, give it a little time, right? I hope so!*

Chris worries me. He always seems preoccupied. He's nice. He needs help. It wasn't easy for him in Vietnam. The least I can do is be a friend. She was nearing home now. *He's such a loner that if I abandon*

*him I don't know what he would do. He's a likable guy most of the time,
though he is a bit possessive. I don't know how far he would carry it.
I've got to find a time to tell him about Paul and me.*

She walked down the hall towards her bedroom to change clothes
and shower, past the fierce golden lion, past the memories.

12

"Nancy, I don't...what...do. It's...scary. Maybe...exaggerating, but...worried." Paul's office was about three steps down the hallway from the reception desk. The new receptionist was Gwen – an attractive, bright young lady. So, as he stepped into the hall intending to go past the reception area and down the hall, he paused, hearing snatches of an unusual phone conversation.

Nancy had been at the firm forever and was the office manager. She was probably the only person the firm couldn't get by without. She was their chief spec writer to the extent that most specs were just boilerplate and needed to be assembled properly. She knew where everything was. She managed all the staff except for the architects and draftspersons. "Just looking out for my people," she would always say. Including now, as it sounded to Paul like Gwen had a problem that really worried Nancy. *Well*, he thought, *nobody better to handle that than Nancy.*

He had recruited Marv, an experienced draftsman from the staff to help him with the bank project, and the other projects he was acquiring. He also had Terry, a bright young man from Dunwoody Technical College in Minneapolis, on his team.

In the middle of March, Paul found out they had won the contract to design the prototype banks. He called Chris to let him know that, so far, their plans were on schedule. Since then, Paul assembled his team, and they were busy drawing, revising, and finalizing some plans.

96

Thad Thistel III is a pain in the ass, thought Paul. Being the head draftsperson had gone to his head long ago. Thin, with a runner's aura, he sometimes seemed to appear out of nowhere. Like now. "Grayson, c'mere!"

"What is it, Thad?"

"It's not often an architect will do his own drawing, so when you do, I'm going to watch it closely. You should leave it to the draftsmen. For example," he unrolled some of the preliminary plans for the prototype banks, "see this roof reinforcement plan on the banks you hotshots are doing?"

"Yes, what about it?" said Paul, warily. He had altered the reinforcing so it was 18 inches shy of covering the vault, thus creating the weak spot he and Chris would exploit in a couple years. He wanted to see if he could get by with it, and getting it in the plans early would help.

"If you check the floor plan and vault overview, you'll see they don't match. A serious error."

Paul moved in closer to pretend to be surprised and to give himself time to think of something. He didn't like standing so close to Thad because he had an odd odor. "Are you sure? I did this one myself."

"Yes, that's what worries me. Check the measurements here—and—here, and let's drop a scale on it. See? Now, like I say, leave the drawing to the pro's. You stick to design, or whatever it is you do. Unless..., no—you wouldn't, never mind." He gave Paul a sidelong glance as he left.

I know the jerk doesn't like me, thought Paul, *as I expected, having jumped right into running my own little projects. But, could he suspect anything for real? He's been here a long time and is excellent at his job, as evidenced by catching this mistake not one in a hundred would find. I know he can say anything to me he wants because my father would back him up. I can't pull the daddy whine on him, and he knows it. Damn!*

Back in his office, with the door shut, he called Chris. "Can you talk now?... Okay, here's the deal. I drew our flaw into the roof reinforcing plan, and our Chief supervising draftsman found it... Yes, that he is. When he passes gas he hits high C. Right now I'm at a loss. Maybe I'll come up with something.... Hmmm, that might work. I'll make the correction so ol' Thad will pass the plans, but I'll keep the roof reinforcing plan with the flaw built in. I'll give that sheet to you and you substitute it after you get the plans... I think that could work. Let's sleep on it.... Okay, we'll meet later."

As he opened the door he noticed it was 5:15 and almost everybody had left. He peeked around the corner and saw Gwen still at the front desk. He approached her and noticed she had been crying. He sat on the edge of her desk and gave her the best brotherly look he could come up with.

She sniffed a bit, "Sorry, I didn't know you were still here."

"Yes, and so are you. You don't have to tell me a thing, but if your problem has to do with work, maybe I can help. I do hold a little sway around here if I want to push it," he chuckled. "What is it?" Silence. "I want to know for selfish reasons, Gwen, we really like your work and attitude here – especially me. Someday I may be in the driver's seat here, and you're just the type of person I want on my team. Nancy will not be here forever. And, yes, she is the best in the world at what she does. So...if you're not happy here, you will look for another job and leave us, plus you'll be miserable while you are here looking for that new job. I don't want that. If it's personal, I've gone on way too long. Just tell me to shut up!"

Gwen looked up into Paul's eyes, looked down, then back up. "I hate to say anything. I'm new here, and, he's been here longer than me."

"Gwen, look, this will stay between us if there is nothing to it. Maybe you are imagining things. Let's talk about it. Just you and me." Paul pulled up a chair.

"Well, okay, here goes. Geez, I feel awful. Anyway, when I first got here a certain employee invited me out for a drink after work. The way he said it, I thought four or five of us were getting together. Turns out it was just him and me. He was a bit suggestive at first, but when you're new you kind of take the 'let it pass' approach. I thought he was kidding or just flirting a little, like guys do. Maybe he was that way with everyone. But, then he got very possessive, demanded another date, and said some not very nice things. I managed to get away and get to my car. I locked the doors and was sitting there shaking, trying to compose myself, then there he was—knocking on my window, and, I think, apologizing from what I could hear. But, I started the car and drove off, maybe over his foot for all I know."

"It would serve him right," remarked Paul, with a concerned look on his face. He observed Gwen who was twisting her hands around a shredded tissue and was almost in tears again. "Gwen, Gwen, it's okay. We're going to get to the bottom of this. How long ago was this?"

"Last week. It's been hard. I don't know what to do. I did talk to Nancy this morning, and she was really upset."

"Yes, rightly so. I did hear snatches of that conversation but didn't know what it was all about. Has anything more happened?"

"Well, yes and no. If we leave the building at the same time, he follows me to my car. I never drive straight home if that happens, but how hard is it to find out where somebody lives? In fact, I'm sure he has parked on my street and watched my house. When he's here in reception he gives me a creepy look. Or, he'll try to find a reason to brush up against me. It's scary."

"I can't imagine what you are going through. Okay, the big question. *Who* is it?"

13

"Man on second and third, two outs, last inning; c'mon Peter, you can do it," Colleen said, half to herself. Colleen was a junior at Rutgers and Peter's fiancée – for almost two whole days now. Peter had pitched all nine innings so far, and Rutgers led 2-1 at their home field.

The count was two balls, two strikes. The pitch...just missed, as the crowd groaned. Peter Williams stepped off the mound, adjusted his cap, stepped back to the rubber, got the catcher's sign, and took a deep breath. *This is it*, he thought as he threw a changeup. The batter must have expected a fastball because he swung early, securing the final out.

The team rushed out to congratulate Peter, while Colleen let out a big yell. "Way to go, Peter!" Now she would navigate the crowd to the parking lot, drive over near the clubhouse, and sit back in her car to wait for Peter.

Sitting back, she had to smile at Peter's proposal. Two days ago he had told her to wait for him by the locker room door because he needed help carrying something. When he came out, he ushered her off to the side, got down on his knee, and, while still in his baseball uniform, asked her to marry him. It wasn't a big surprise – they had already been discussing their future plans. What did surprise her was the whole team, in their uniforms, running out the locker room door and surrounding them right after she said yes. Whooping and yelling, they made a big spectacle. It didn't help that she was crying with happiness, but she soon got that under control. They all went to the ball field where they took pictures of her and Peter at all the bases, pitcher's mound, and then made them cross home plate together. "The biggest home run of my life," Peter had remarked.

Now, he was coming across the parking lot to her car with a big smile on his face. He got in her car and gave her a big kiss. "Honey, I've got some news. This morning I got a call that my first choice internship was approved. And, after the internship, if all goes as expected, it will turn into a full-time job. I'll be able to stay in the area while you complete your degree."

"Peter, that is great news! Wow, what a day so far, huh?"

"Couldn't be better. I was thinking, and want to know what you think, about setting a wedding date now that my future is more solid."

"You mean get married *before* I finish school?"

"I know we planned on waiting, but with this new turn of events, why not consider it?" mused Peter, "It couldn't happen tomorrow, 'cuz it takes, what, a good week to plan a wedding? Just kidding! How long *does* it take?"

"Let's think about this for a couple days before we decide. Wow, it is exciting, though, to think of getting married sooner."

"Okay. I'm going to go for a quick bike ride, shower up, and then we'll have a special dinner to celebrate our good luck. Hey, and the big win on the diamond!"

I'll be using up my last rifle, thought Chris, *but I guess that's what they're for*. While out west last year he had purchased two rifles: one in Reno and one in Laramie, both at gun shows. Hard to trace, he knew. The Reno-bought rifle was long gone, and soon the Laramie rifle would be, too.

He thought long and hard about how to convey to the politicians the same feelings that the families of the men sent to the useless war in Vietnam were feeling. The executions of the responsible politicians was payback, for sure. But, it didn't have the same effect. Those executed were soon forgotten, except by a small circle of family members.

So, here he was in a small, wooded area just outside of Rutgers University, next to a popular bike path. His rental car behind him parked off to the side of a seldom-used road. He held his Laramie bought rifle firmly in his left hand. After researching Senator Williams of Maryland, an outspoken supporter of the war, he found he had a son, Peter, and daughter, Barbara. Peter was a senior at Rutgers and a star baseball player. The daughter, Chris didn't care about. He knew the son was also an avid biker and almost always biked on this path right before dinner.

This would be his easiest execution, and his hardest; so hard, he hadn't even told Harlow anything about this one. As far as she was concerned, he was looking at used equipment and going to a couple of construction auctions. Hopefully she wouldn't connect him to this event, or if she did, she would see it his way. Hard to tell. It was a tough one. Technically, a piece of cake: the boy would be an easy target. Hard though, because the boy, himself, had done nothing wrong. But, it *was* war, and thousands of innocent young men had been sacrificed in Vietnam – over 40,000 to date. This one would be sacrificed to make a point and maybe help draw this god-forsaken war to a close.

He stood quietly, waiting for the lone cyclist. Fifteen minutes later, it was all over, and Chris was already ten miles from campus. In another ten minutes, he would get to the bridge and throw the rifle into the river unseen, drop off the rental car, then walk three blocks to a shopping mall where he had left his van. He had a few things to do on the way home, but would be back in three days.

As expected, there was a loud outcry over the death of Senator Williams' son, Peter. Not as expected was a letter printed in the *Washington Post*, purportedly from the killer of Peter Williams. Since the letter was postmarked before the killing had occurred, the newspaper had to assume it was the real thing. The letter read:

I am sorry for the death of an innocent young man at Rutgers University. It was unnecessary – just like the over 40,000 American young people who died in Vietnam was unnecessary. Senator Williams' family will grieve forever for young Peter, as will his friends and acquaintances. Their lives will never be the same. Senator, that is the same feeling 40,000 other American families have had. How do you like it?

Here's another feeling. Each month I will execute another child of a congressperson until this war ends. And, if you guard them so well that I can't, that's okay. I will keep tally. Someday you will let your guard down, and I will catch up. Now you will know the feeling of dread every family goes through as they pray that their soldier gets through another day in a worthless war. You will live each day in fear, as you have put thousands of families in that same fear.

vivre et laisser vivre

14

"I am not what you think I am. I have done great work here for as long as this firm has existed," whined Thad Thistel III.

"Thad, listen to me," said Randolph Grayson. "Nobody doubts your work. In fact it makes me sick to think of having to replace you. But, it is in the best interests of all concerned that you leave the firm immediately."

Paul, Nancy and Allen were also in attendance, but deferred to Randolph to handle this. They were there as witnesses and to answer any questions. Paul met with Nancy the morning after his talk with Gwen. Nancy was happy to have some help in the matter, and Paul was thankful. That way it wouldn't look like a solo vendetta against Thad. He kept extra quiet.

Paul and Nancy knew they were in one of those "he said—she said" situations. Then, Nancy had a flash of brilliance. She suggested they look deeper into why several other women at the office had quit over the past five years. Nancy always wondered why there was such high turnover among her staff. She carefully vetted each of the girls herself, and had given them extra attention and help as they got started. Still, too many left for no apparent reason.

Paul suggested they dig in their own pockets and hire a private detective to locate three or four of the most suspicious cases of quitting with no reason. The idea being, if Thad had hit on Gwen, he had probably done it before. He went to a police precinct and asked for the name of a respected private eye and got two names. He picked one, and he was willing to try to track down four of the girls that Nancy named. That in itself wasn't too hard, as they were in the phone book or were easily located with just a couple phone calls. The hard part would be to get them to admit, if it was the case, being harassed by Thad.

Fortunately, three of the girls were happy to write a letter describing what happened to them, including the threats of what would happen if they squealed. As one of the girls said, "In retrospect, I think of him as a harmless pervert. I was more concerned that I would lose my job than that he would actually do me any harm. And, since jobs of my type weren't that hard to find, it was just easier to hunt for a new job while I was working at the firm, then move on. I felt bad for leaving Nancy. She was a great boss, but I just couldn't tell her. Who would believe *me*, the new girl?"

After getting the letters in hand, Paul and Nancy requested a meeting with Randolph, who wanted Allen in on it, too. The four of them agreed they should call Thad in immediately, show him the letters and ask for his resignation right away. He would have to sign a no-compete clause and promise, in writing, never to contact any of the women involved or to cause them any discomfort. If he would agree to that, there would be three month's severance pay and no complaint to the police. They had a quick meeting with the firm's lawyer who drafted the contract.

So, here they were in Randolph's office, with the ball in Thad's court. "Those girls led me on. I could tell they were enjoying the attention."

"Thad," Paul said, as he couldn't stand it any longer, "you are messed up and need help. But, you're done here. And, if we hear of any more trouble, we're going to find more girls, and they will be glad to put you away. We have signed letters from these three girls. Once they found out they weren't the only ones, they were ready to hire a lawyer and have you hung from the highest tree. We really had to do some talking to keep that from happening, and I'm not sure we're even doing the right thing."

"Well, I can see you've all turned on me, so I wouldn't want to work here anymore anyway. Give me those papers to sign and my severance check and you'll never see me again!"

Allen anticipated this outcome and had the check ready. "Thad, I can't let you in the office on your own," Randolph said, "so if it's okay with you, I'll escort you to your desk so you can get your personal things, then escort you to the door."

"I'm fine on my own. I know the way out."

"It wasn't really a request, Thad. Oh, key please. By the way, your work was always top notch. I'll miss that. Let's get your belongings."

As Paul, Nancy and Allen stood, Thad stopped at the door to look back at them one more time, then said to Paul, "You're up to something, college boy. I'm going to keep my eye on you."

"That's enough!" said Randolph. "Let's go!"

15

"Are you ready, Sara?" whispered Dr. Rodney McKenny. A silent affirmative nod was the only answer.

The meeting room at Veterans Hospital was white, clinical, and efficient looking, almost as a reminder that this is a hospital and don't you forget it. The metal folding chairs were dented and worn. Fourteen chairs wide and ten rows deep, about one fourth of them occupied. Every three months, it was the custom to call a general staff meeting involving all administration, all department heads, all head nurses, and an assortment of other personnel. Director Anderson was of the unshakeable belief that the hospital was one happy family. Further, that if everyone in the hospital knew what was going on, it would continue to be one happy family.

"Dr. McKenny, what's happening on your ward?" Dr. McKenny stood up briskly, looked around the austere room and announced that Nurse Sara Forsyth was going to start his report.

Sara stood up, nervously cleared her throat and started her report. "Thank you Dr. McKenny," giving him a nod and a quick look. She wondered how many, if any, of the people in this room knew of her relationship with the good doctor. "As you know from the previous reports, we have a Vietnam veteran who has been with us for about eighteen months. The first five months he was cataleptic. He also had severe spinal damage, the extent we could not tell partly because of his mental state. About two months ago," she continued, more confident now, "we detected some eye movement, then some head movement. We've worked very hard with Sergeant Tonger, and he has responded beautifully. He can talk now, ask questions, even carry on a conversation, and respond to affection." She blushed slightly as she realized how this might sound. But, either the audience was not listening or did not have the imagination she gave them credit for. "He has no movement in his legs, but has some sensation there. He apparently has nightmares several times a week. The attendants report him thrashing his arms about, mumbling and screaming, and sweating a great deal. We are working on that."

She continued, "He seems confused about his past. He has only one living relative, his senile dad is in Baltimore, and we have no one from his family to help orient him. We think—er, that is Dr. McKenny thinks," she gestured toward him and gave him a professional smile, "that if the psych department could set up a series of visits from a doctor, nurse, even an orderly, over several months, to ask him questions about himself, and repeat this ten to fifteen times, Sergeant Tonger will reveal more and more details of what happened to him." She gave the details as to when and where to meet with him, and how to report any new information.

After the meeting she excused herself from the group, made some rounds and was waiting in Dr. McKenny's office when he walked in. He put down his clipboard, reached for two cups and poured both full from the coffee mate on his credenza. "Sara, you did a fine job," as he extended his right arm offering her a coffee, "and I've got news. Dr. Lanyard, the neurologist, thinks it's about time to get to work on Sergeant Tonger's legs. He's checked the latest X-rays and other tests, and he thinks we've got a 20 percent chance to improve his condition."

"Great. Just great! I've got a feeling we're going to pull this one off. Sometimes it's depressing to know we are more or less a warehouse." She looked up quickly to see if she could get a sense of disapproval from Dr. McKenny, but saw him nodding his head. "So, when we get one with a ray of hope, we're going to push it for all it's worth. In fact, Mandy, his physical therapist, and I both sensed an awakening in Sergeant Tonger. She will be as eager as I to make this happen. We'll be a great team. Team Tonger!"

She didn't dare reveal that she had grown to like Sergeant Tonger quite a lot. It was probably natural, since she was spending many of her spare hours talking with him, helping him work his upper body, and being a companion. When she first started her affair with Dr. McKenny, they had spent a lot of time together, but he was back to his routine of many hours at the hospital. To be fair, he did have a lot of responsibility. But, that did leave her with time alone. She chose to spend some of it with Sergeant Tonger. She knew he did like her. Of course, that's a common syndrome among recovering patients, to fall in "love" with their nurse. But, to fall in love with your patient? *Be careful*, she thought.

She left her office. Her duty shift was over, and as usual, she headed for room 306. Jim was in bed, pulling on the weights they had rigged up. "Hi," he knew it was her without even looking. He let the rings up easy, turned and looked at her with a big smile. He always enjoyed this time of the day, at least during the week. Sara had been very faithful at stopping most every day. He looked at her in her nurse's uniform and his heart beat faster. She was the one who drove him on. Not a very big girl, maybe 5'-6", brunette, blue eyes, shapely, but she had something special he couldn't put his finger on. *There are a lot of things I can't put my finger on right now*, he thought. *So many nagging feelings. I guess I need to be patient, as they keep telling me.*

He was going to recover fully, so he could treat her like the special lady she was. They would take walks, go skiing, visit Disneyworld. Anywhere – anything she wanted. She didn't know this yet, of course. In his current condition, he had no right to expect her to see any future in him. So, he had worked doubly hard at the weights and at the mental part, too. He was getting stronger in the upper body, but not much had progressed with his legs or memory.

16

DECEMBER 1973
CHRISTMAS

"Here we are," announced Paul. He pulled the big, black Buick Riviera to the curb and shut it down. It was toasty warm inside – a stark contrast to the cold and crisp outside. Ellen had talked Paul into a short Christmas Eve hike in Hiawatha Park. Paul reluctantly agreed. The park was covered in darkness by this hour, yet the twinkling stars and half-moon brightened up the freshly fallen snow, introducing a lightness to the winter evening.

Paul put his hand behind Ellen as he turned towards her. "You look radiant," he said, as he pulled her closer until his lips found hers. She reached her hand behind his head and pulled him even closer. It was a lingering, tantalizing kiss. Paul liked it. He liked Ellen a lot, too. Although she was normally bright, sparkling and cheerful, he found when they were alone like this, she was often quieter and reflective and not very intense. Her mood seemed different tonight. Breaking away and opening her door, Ellen said breathlessly, "C'mon Paul, let's get started on this winter wonderland hike."

"You asked for it. You want to hike? We'll hike," Paul laughed.

"Isn't this grand?" Ellen gestured towards the park and its lake. She encircled his arm with both of hers as they started a meandering walk down the path to the lake, and then eventually around it. A consistent flurry of snow was falling, draping itself over the landscape and balancing delicately on the tree branches. Every once in a while, a slight breeze would topple nature's handiwork, and it would start all over. At the far end of the lake, a half-dozen teenagers were skating circles and figure eights, punctuating their ice design work with occasional laughter.

Paul and Ellen walked in silence, content to drink in their first Christmas Eve together in this picturesque setting, sharing feelings without exchanging words. The pace was leisurely and reflective.

Steve and I used to skate in that exact spot, thought Ellen. *This is the third Christmas without him, but I'm not nearly as lonely this Christmas*. She gave Paul a gentle hug on his arm as they continued. He looked in her eyes, guessing correctly what was going on. It wasn't the first time. He'd give her all the room she needed. He knew how much her brother meant to her and could only guess how hard it had to be.

"Christmas used to be a hard time for me," said Ellen." "Maybe I'm stubborn, or old fashioned, but I could never get interested in Christmas parties. The birth of Christ seems a poor reason to drag out the booze bottles. But, to each their own. "Paul," she paused, "how did you usually spend your Christmas Eves?"

"The usual, I guess. We would go to my Grandparents' house in Wayzata, have supper, and listen to the grown-ups talk about the good ol' days," he chuckled. "It was okay. That was the one night my father stayed with us the whole night."

"I hardly know your father. The times I've been to your house he— uh, well, I don't know, seems cool and formal. Does he approve of me? Or maybe he doesn't say anything to you?"

"Not much, really, Ellen. Actually I don't see that much of him. I've got my own entrance and den and bed and bath, so sometimes two or three days go by that I don't see him at all. Not even at work.

113

Approval?" Paul paused. The snow was coming down thicker, but the wind had stilled. They were around to where the skaters had been practicing their make-believe Olympics, but they were gone. The snow had a muffling effect. Objects were muted and softly shaped. Sounds were muted and distant. The moon reflected its soft, yellow glow off the snowy ice just to their right. Paul led them a few steps into a triangle of evergreen trees, faced Ellen, put his arms around her waist and pulled her close. She willingly gave herself to his embrace. Lips touching lightly at first, then turning into a harder, more urgent kiss. Soon their lips separated, but Ellen held tight, putting her cheek next to his. The warmth and closeness giving her a full, bursting feeling. She could feel a path of warmth course from her cheeks to her slightly weak knees, warming her entire being. A little, brown and white cottontail rabbit stopped about 20 feet away, sat up and looked towards Ellen. She smiled and winked at it, and it went on its way, stopping every 20 feet or so to sit up and check out the surroundings before bounding over a small, snow-covered hill.

"Is that approval enough?" Paul pulled away and looked deep into her green eyes with a sincere smile on his face.

"More than enough," she laughed. "Whew! C'mon, let's get back."

The plan was to make popcorn in the fireplace of Paul's den. His parents would join them for a short time, sharing a bottle of wine and some fudge Ellen made at her apartment.

Paul led Ellen through the terrace door so they could go directly to Paul's den. The fire they started earlier was almost out. Ellen was handing some logs to Paul when there was a knock at the den door.

"Anybody here?" The door opened to frame Randolph and Marcie Grayson.

"Sure. Hi. Come in." replied Paul. "We'll get this fire going, and then we'll treat you to a few goodies."

Paul was hunched down by the fire, and Ellen was next to him with the bellows.

"Hi," she said perkily, "nice to see you again." As she turned to see them, she noticed they were both dressed pretty formally. Turning back, she noticed Paul's back slightly heaving up and down. The elder Graysons were still a ways away checking out some book titles at the bookcase near the door. "What's the matter with you?" she whispered.

"You can't be serious," he could hardly control his giggling.

"What are you talking about?" she whispered, half mad.

"Look at them. Remember when you called them Randy and Macy?" He continued out the side of his mouth. The giggling was contagious. She remembered the first time she referred to his parents that way. She was just being playful and meant no disrespect. Paul had laughed and laughed about that. Even weeks later, he would chuckle and she would know why. He had to explain to her they were the most formal, reserved couple he ever knew. It was always "Randolph and Marcie." They were wound tight. Prim and proper... always.

He had told Ellen, having rarely seen his parents in anything but "proper attire," her new names for them painted this ludicrous picture in his mind of two down and outers with old, tattered clothes, disheveled hair, and holes in the soles of their tennis shoes. He didn't know why, but it had.

She jabbed him in the ribs, gathered herself, and stood up to face his parents, while he dabbed unobtrusively at his eyes.

"It sure is a beautiful night. Paul and I went for a walk in Hiawatha Park. It is gorgeous!" she said, as she prepared the wine.

"Yes, it is nice," said Marcie as she accepted a glass for her and Randolph. Ellen refilled drinks as the light conversation continued with all participating. Paul made popcorn, and compliments were handed out on the great fudge. The atmosphere felt a little strained, but reasonably comfortable.

Ellen promised herself that she would work on her self-esteem and self-confidence. She wanted to be rid of her lingering feelings of inadequacy. Paul and she had discussed this, and he called to her attention an excellent quote from Eleanor Roosevelt: "Nobody can make you feel inferior without your consent." She liked that. It was something she could relate to, and it was working tonight. It was a nice evening. Christmas Eve – a special one.

She settled down on the floor in front of Paul's easy chair with her back between his legs, leaning on the chair with her knees drawn up and held in place by her arms wrapping around. Her white cashmere sweater was changing colors reflecting the dancing rhythm of the fire. The conversation had dwindled as all four felt comfortable watching and listening to the fire work its magic. A contemplative, relaxed mood had settled in as the wine and room warmth took over. Ellen felt good. She belonged.

She turned and looked up at Paul with a request, spoken softly. "What?" he whispered, coming out of his reverie and leaning forward a bit. "Oh, okay. Good idea." He went to his cabinet and removed his guitar. Warming up a little he sat on the hassock, facing the three. "Now we are going to have a little Christmas carol sing-along."

"Paul," his mother scoffed, "you know Randolph and I, well..." she looked at Randolph with a little smile, "we haven't sung in years. You young people go ahead. It is getting late for us. But, I would like to hear a couple Christmas carols. How about you, Randolph?" He seemed very relaxed and quickly agreed.

"Any requests?" Paul asked Ellen.

"No, you're playing the music, you start."

After *White Christmas* and several other Christmas carols, Mrs. Grayson said, "Say, you two sure can sing! This is better than Lawrence Welk. And, that means it's good! C'mon Randolph, let's try a couple songs. It looks like they should be able to carry us," she laughed quite heartily.

After *Let it Snow* and two more songs together, all four were laughing and clapping, really enjoying themselves. "Well," Randolph said, taking a couple of deep breaths, "we better get to bed, Ma," he laughed as he looked at his wife and took her hand. "These young folks plumb tuckered me out. And, it is after midnight."

"Yes, I had a lot of fun. Paul, Ellen, thanks for inviting us." She looked at Paul and took both his hands in hers. Then, she stepped to Ellen, who was standing next to Paul with arms at her sides. Marcie put one hand on each of Ellen's upper arms, kissed her on the cheek and said, "Merry—Merry Christmas, Ellen," and turned to leave the room.

Randolph stepped quickly forward, clasped Paul's right hand in both of his and gave an enthusiastic handshake. "Yes, I had a great time, too." Turning and taking Ellen's hand he said, "Ellen, you are welcome anytime. We are proud to know you." Then, hurrying to catch up with his wife, he waved a quick good night.

Paul returned to the couch, sat down on the edge, and started to play his guitar, humming a Christmas tune. Ellen sat down beside him, leaned back, clasped her hands behind her head, kicked her shoes off and leaned back even more, a wide happy smile on her face.

"You know, I think Mother and Father, or Randy and Macy, as you like to call them," he said, ducking an incoming pillow, "sort of like you. Course you are a likable sort." Paul set his guitar alongside the couch and leaned back with Ellen.

"I like them too," Ellen replied softly, dreamily. "I was just thinking, this is the best Christmas Eve I've had in a long time. I am so fulfilled and happy. You treat me so good. And..." she headed for the shopping bag she had stashed in the corner by her purse. She returned with a brightly wrapped package. "This is your Christmas present for putting up with me almost a whole year!" She was laughing lightly. "Go on, open it."

It was a beautiful sky-blue knit sweater from Sweden. Thank you's were said and accepted.

"Now you sit back." Paul produced an envelope which he gave to Ellen, with a bit of flourish. "There's some explaining that goes with this, but you open it first, then we'll talk."

"What in the world could it be?" She asked looking at him with a puzzled expression. Tearing the envelope open she withdrew its contents. "An airline ticket to Hawaii?" she gasped. "What...?"

"I'll explain." They were both sitting on the edge of the couch by now.

"This ticket is for February. I'd love to go – you know I would. But, Mrs. Thoms has scheduled my vacation for April, and she won't change her mind."

"Would you like to bet?"

"You didn't—she didn't?!"

"You bet she did. My mother is probably among your best customers, so I had her do a little persuading. Your vacation is rescheduled. Actually Ellen, I'm taking a lot for granted here, I know. I remember you telling me how much you wanted to see Hawaii, especially after you had that four-hour layover there on your way back from Japan. I would like very much to go, also. Why not you and I go together? We're adults. We enjoy each other's company. I think it would be terrific."

Ellen was thinking of all the possible complications. Am I ready for a more intense relationship? What would Steve have said? I'll bet he would say I should go and have a good time. "This is for ten days, right?" She was looking at the ticket thinking of how much she would like to go, but knowing she could not accept a ten-day paid trip.

"Yes, ten days. But, before you make up your mind, there is a hitch."

"Let me guess," she interrupted, "on each island they only had one room left and we have to share it."

"No," Paul laughed, "but it's a good idea. Actually, I've made all the reservations. Your room is reserved for you in your name and, ah, well, you'll have to pay for it yourself."

"You bet I will," replied Ellen, "and I'll pay for my meals. Well, you can take me out once or twice if you want, but I want to pay my share!" She paused, "You're not kidding me on this, are you?"

"Absolutely not. Boy scouts honor!"

"Okay, I'm game. Sounds like fun. You better drive me home fast. I have planning to do." They both got up together. "But first," she took Paul into her arms and pressed her lips to his, their bodies coming firmly together. She felt they were as one. Overflowing, heartfelt, loving. Steve would approve. Merry Christmas.

17

JANUARY / FEBRUARY 1974
SGT. TONGER

January 7 was another frustrating day for Sgt. James E. Tonger. As he was dragging his legs behind him on the parallel bars, he was wondering what was really going on. Yes, there was feeling in his legs and he could actually move them, but he was nowhere near walking. It seemed almost hopeless. But nonetheless, there was something driving him on. He knew he had unfinished business, but didn't know what it was. He couldn't remember the accident or anything before. That was just as frustrating as not being able to walk. He had to do something.

The one good thing was Sara. He enjoyed her company so much. She seemed to enjoy his. Why else would she visit him almost every day after work? He finished his workout and, with help from his therapist, plopped into his wheelchair and went to the dining area. It was good to get out of his room and visit with others. The bad thing was the talk often turned to "going home," or the next visit from "mom and dad," or the next visit from "my wife."

As far as he knew, his dad was in an old folk's home in Baltimore and wouldn't know him anyway. That didn't seem quite right, but a lot of things didn't seem right.

"Jim, how was your day?" asked Sara as she held his forearm. She had once again stopped in after work.

"Slow going," replied Jim, "but what else am I going to do? I don't seem to be making that much progress even with the extra sessions I

120

asked for, and I still don't remember a thing. I know I should, but I just can't."

"I can only imagine how hard it is. I've seen a lot in this hospital, including almost miracles. You are making progress. I remember what you were like when you came here. You're miles past that, thank goodness!"

"Sara, I need a big favor. I know some patients have gone home on short weekends or have made other trips. I want you to arrange for me to take a trip to Baltimore to see my dad, and I want you to come along. I know he is senile, but I have to see if that will help me to start to remember."

"That might be possible, Jim. When we have our group consult about our patients, there is concern…" she looked around and started talking more quietly, "about your memory. Look, I'm not supposed to share anything from these meetings, so don't say anything. Your doctor can tell you what he wants, but not me. Anyway, we did talk about trying something different. This could be one avenue. I think it's worth a shot. Don't get me wrong, it is not unusual in cases like yours for the memory to come around, so it's a long way from hopeless, even now. Sometimes something will be the trigger that starts it coming back very fast. Sometimes it's a slow piece at a time. You'll get there," she reassured.

"Have you got more time?"

"Sure."

"Grab that chair and pull it by old ironsides here." He took her hand in his, she didn't pull away. *That's good*, he thought. "You mean a lot to me. You're here almost every day after work, and that means more than you'll ever know. I'm also sure every one of your other patients feel the same way. You're beautiful, smart, nice, caring—I could go on, but you might slap me. Anyway, um, um, why are you still single?"

She looked at him, then looked out the window for a few seconds, then said,

"That's none of your business, but since I like you, I'll answer," she laughed. "I'm not that old yet, thank you very much, so there is still time. I had the love of my life while in nurses training, but he finished college before I did. He got his dream job in Phoenix, and our relationship went the way of most long-distance romances. It took me awhile to get over that, *if* I am over it. Also, this job is very consuming. Maybe someday. I would ask you about your love life, but you wouldn't remember. Ha!"

"Very funny," chuckled Jim. "If you're still available when I am more of a man, I'd like to take you to the finest restaurant in Baltimore. Actually, I'd like to take you on the vacation of your life, but that might be pushing it."

She couldn't very well tell him about her romance with Dr. McKenny, if it indeed was a romance. At first it was exciting, and she still liked him a lot, but it seemed like he was taking her more for granted every week. Then there was the age difference, and marriage didn't seem like a topic of any conversation. But still...

Sara realized she had been holding Jim's hand this whole time, gave it a squeeze, and let go. "You know," she said, with a light sigh, "I might just take you up on that offer. Be careful what you wish for."

"Which offer?" Jim asked, with a little smirk.

"That's for me to know. Bye. See you tomorrow."

February 5, 1974

The hospital van wasn't the smoothest ride in America, but Jim, Sara, and an aide were on their way to Baltimore. Sara had finally got the okay for the trip and had made the arrangements as quick as she could, which wasn't all that quick in VA land. Jim's wheelchair was in the back, and Jim and Sara settled in the second seat as the aide drove. Along the way, Jim managed to hold Sara's hand while they talked, unseen by the driver. She did give him a little look when he took it, but didn't pull it away.

They arrived at the nursing home, put Jim in the wheelchair— actually he could almost do it himself now—and went inside. Jim had low expectations, but still found himself very nervous. They were expected, so an LPN took Jim and Sara to his dad's room. Mr. Tonger was sitting, tilted over, in the only chair in the dingy room, eyes vacant.

Jim wheeled over and said, "Dad?" Swallowed hard, "Dad?" No response.

The nurse softly said, "He hasn't talked in years, sorry. I was here when he first came and he was somewhat responsive, but that was a while ago. Records show his wife, your mother, died many years ago, and you are the only living relative. Actually, now that you are here, could you give us any names from his past?"

Jim's mind was far away, so he did not respond.

Sara said to the nurse, "He hasn't got his memory back from his accident. We were hoping this might help him to remember something. We'll have to wait and see."

"Jim, you want to go, or you want to sit here awhile? Jim?"

"Let's go, I think this was a bad idea." Jim's eyes were brimming with tears.

123

18

FEBRUARY 1973
HAWAII

The day broke cold and clear in Minneapolis. Ellen could feel the cold go right through her blue 'Brooks Brothers' coat as she carried her two, baby blue Samsonite suitcases to Paul's car.

"Forty-two below."

"What?" said Ellen.

"Forty-two below zero. That's the wind chill. Heard it on the way over. And, a good morning to you," said Paul, slipping her luggage in the back seat after giving her a warm kiss.

They made the Northwest Airlines check-in desk with time to spare. Soon, they were on board with Paul settling into his window seat. "Oh, I can hardly wait," Ellen said, as she leaned across Paul and peered through the small window. "This is going to be so much fun!" Paul had explained about the islands and some of the sights they would see. She had already done her research, but let him go on anyway. Maybe she would learn something new. The flight was long, but uneventful. They dozed and talked of many things. Paul thought how Ellen had a way of making him feel very special. As they started their approach, Ellen watched carefully through the window. They had changed seats about halfway over, so she had a great view of the tropical coastline during the descent. "It looks like a scene from a movie," Ellen said excitedly, as she took Paul's hand and gave it a squeeze.

After stretching their legs and exiting the plane, they hurried through the wide open airport to get their luggage. Bags in hand, they traipsed to the rental car counter and were on their way to the Royal Sands Hotel.

"I can't believe this," squealed Ellen. "It's, it's so balmy. And, look at the palm trees." Paul was busy looking for the hotel, following the directions given him at the car rental counter. "There it is." Ellen pointed it out. A new high-rise – an attractive looking building. "It's right on the beach!"

They each registered for their rooms, which were connecting, and had the Porter bring the luggage up. Paul was just putting his clothes in a drawer when he heard a soft rap at the connecting door. "Can I come in?" smiled Ellen.

"My house is yours, oh Princess of Hawaii." He took her in his arms, gave her a warm kiss, and held her tight.

"Have you seen the balcony? C'mon, you have to see this. "She took him by the arm, opened the sliding door, and together they stepped out onto a small lanai. The white sands of Waikiki beach stretched for miles to the left, all the way over to where Diamond Head, an old volcanic crater, jetted up into the sky. To the right, the beach showed here and there through palm trees and a variety of lush tropical growth. Straight ahead lay the blue-green Pacific, rolling and fighting the shore with large frothy waves. The trade winds blew a steady breeze into their faces carrying the scent of sea and salt to their nostrils. The air was warm and fresh.

"Did you ever wonder how many miles those waves rolled before they got here?" asked Paul, "Or, how long that breeze has been blowing without touching a human? Guess it's kind of silly—no answers."

"Well, waves don't really travel, they just kind of undulate," said Ellen as she got a questioning look from Paul. "Hey, I read up on this stuff—ah—never mind. Forget it. We are on vacation. God, it's beautiful. What say we get our bathing suits on, grab a couple towels and some sunscreen and head for that magnificent beach? Shake off some of this jet lag and unpack later. It's 3:30 now, so at 3:45 come over to my room and help me carry some beach stuff. Okay?" She was opening her door.

"I could come over early," he said to her disappearing back.

She leaned back, "That's what you think, Buster," she laughed and closed the door behind her.

They claimed a spot on Waikiki's white sands. Ellen took off her terry cloth cover and revealed a slightly tan body.

"Hey, no fair," said Paul. "You've been catching a few hours under the ol' sunlamp." He was appraising her from his side view as she was heading for the ocean. He liked what he saw. Even though she was one of the few on the fairly crowded beach with a one piece suit, she was a striking figure. Fairly tall for a woman, well proportioned, shapely legs and a well-developed bust-line. *I knew all that,* he thought, but had never seen her in a bathing suit. He hurried to catch up with her, his feet racing across the hot, fine, Waikiki sand. He grabbed her hand and pulled her into an easy run with him. "Here we go," he said as they ran into the rolling Pacific waves until up to their thighs, making it hard to continue running. Paul dove headfirst into a big wave. Ellen wasn't ready, and the crashing wave threw her back towards the beach, momentarily holding her under.

She came up gasping, coughing, and kicking. "Paul, Paul, where did you go?" she gasped as she twirled around. He was right there and led her back to their towels, laughing and giving her a bad time. She was still coughing and wiping her eyes. "Well, you could have warned me!"

she said, half mad.

"Hey, don't look at me," he said, kneeling beside her, palms up and shrugging. "You're a big girl, remember? You can take care of yourself. Now lie down and I'll put some sunscreen on your tender, Minnesota back."

Paul gently applied sunscreen to her shoulders and arms with a massage type motion. He could feel her tenseness melt as he moved down her back, just under the suit a little, then down to her legs. He was working on the top of her legs when she said, "Watch it Mac, you could get arrested. Your turn anyway." She sat up and gave him a little shove on his chest, he fell backward and rolled over.

Ellen's hands were surprisingly strong as she worked the sunscreen into his arms, back and legs. He relaxed as he thought of Ellen. Five foot eight, green eyes, sincere, trusting, yet an awareness that would keep her from getting in over her head. A lot to like. *Somebody I could spend a lot of time with. Maybe the rest of my life.*

"Ellen?"

"What?" she said dreamily.

"Do you think it's ever okay to take the law into your own hands? I mean like if a big wrong is done to a person or group, do you think they have a right, maybe even an obligation, to redress that wrong?" He turned toward her, laying on his side with his elbow in the warm sand and his chin on his hand.

She moved back a little and curled her legs around behind her. Reaching for her straw hat she said, "I don't know. What do you mean specifically?" She looked into his blue eyes and wondered where he was going with this.

People were close by, the beach was fairly crowded, but it was like being alone together. Nobody else cared what two young people said to each other on a sandy beach on a small island out in the blue Pacific. Not an ounce of fat on that body, she thought as she continued to look him over. Muscular, but slender, wavy black hair, handsome face. Nice guy. *You got it all baby.* He was looking down, studying his toes. A feeling of jealousy rose up within her again! *Watch that,* her own thoughts warned. *Just have fun. I deserve it. Do I, really?* The thoughts kept coming. *Yes, I do! Okay, I will.*

"Like Steve." He paused and looked at her eyes for a reaction. She looked away, grabbed a handful of sand and let it hourglass its way out of her hand. She looked back at him like she expected him to continue. "I know you miss him. He had to mean more to you than you let on. I can sense when he's in your heart. You can be melancholy, reflective, almost pliable, at times. But, since you've got a little stubborn streak you're not too pliable." He laughed as he stood up and brushed the sand from his legs. Reaching down he took her hands in his and pulled her to her feet. "We're supposed to be having fun, not heavy conversation. Let's go back and get dressed for dinner. I'm taking you out!"

Dinner was fabulous. Between courses they talked of the sights they had seen and made plans for tomorrow. It included shopping for a new bathing suit for Ellen as she had wanted an authentic Hawaiian two piece.

Enjoying their after-dinner drink at the beach restaurant, Ellen said, "Paul go on with the thoughts you started on the beach. I'm interested."

"Are you sure?" She nodded while sipping her Mai-Tai. "I know it's painful to talk about Steve but it makes a point. We could almost say he—or it could have been me—gave his life for nothing. A no-win, pulled punches war in a country governed by corrupt leadership. I mean, it didn't make any sense, yet those congressmen and politicians wouldn't let go. They kept sacrificing our brave young people because of their ineptness. They should pay!" He had gotten louder than he intended.

Ellen grabbed his raised, clenched fists in her hands and gently, but firmly coaxed them to the table. She gave a sweet smile to the older couple sitting to their right, who seemed quite nosey. They went back to not talking to each other.

Paul shifted uneasily in his chair. He had said more than he wanted. He couldn't let this happen again. Nobody, including Ellen, should know of his intense dislike for what happened in Nam. "Sorry, I got a little carried away. And, I don't mean Steve died for nothing. He was part of a team, doing what had to be done, like most soldiers. I would do it again, too, because that's what a soldier does. Anyway, you know it's like 3:00 a.m. in Minneapolis? I'm bushed. You ready?"

"I forgot about that much time change. You're right," said Ellen. "Let's get back to our royal quarters." They were quiet on the way back. At the doors to their rooms, which were about three feet apart, Paul enveloped Ellen in his arms. She returned his hug, gave him a quick peck on the cheek, and slipped into her room. "I'll call your room in the morning," she said as the door swept closed.

She sat on her bed with her head down, a trickle of tears falling. *I still can't talk about Steve without ending up like this*, she thought. *And, I am so lucky to have found Paul. Yet I feel I am betraying Steve when I let myself feel close to him. I know Steve would want me to be happy. And, Paul looks so much like Steve it gets complicated. I don't know. Maybe I need help.* Wiping her tears, she readied for bed.

Their second day on the island was set aside to recover from travel, to just do anything or nothing. And, they did – a little time on the beach, a walk through the International Marketplace, where Ellen found just the right bathing suit, a hike arm-in-arm through Kapioloni Park, taking pictures at the Kodak Hula show, a tour through Bishop Museum, and more time on the beach. "An incredible way to live," Ellen told Paul. "Almost paradise."

That night they took in the Don Ho show and afterward went dancing. They found out they were both excellent dancers. Whether they were tired or had one too many drinks, it was hard to tell, but Ellen found herself pressing close to Paul while slow dancing to "Could I have this dance..." He had wrapped his arms around her, and she liked it very much. They were barely moving. He tipped her chin up and moved his lips to hers. She returned the lingering kiss. A warm feeling at her center. The music stopped, but she kept dancing until Paul released her.

Paul could tell she was a little dizzy. "Ellen," he chided her softly as he guided her to their table. "I told you that three Mai-Tais and one Chi-Chi would be too much for you," he chuckled.

"Yes," she slurred a little, "but they were soooo good." She saw his look of concern and started to giggle. The harder she tried to stop the worse it got. Finally tears were running down her cheek, and Paul got caught up in it, too. He had never seen her laugh like this before, but then he had never seen her intoxicated before either.

Finally, she got herself under control, took a deep breath, looked around and said, "God, isn't this fantastic!" They were on an outdoor patio with the warm tropical breeze blowing incessantly. The surf was making its own music less than one hundred yards away. No flies, no mosquitos and no cold weather.

The band was taking a break. There was just a two-foot-high brick planter separating them from the beach. "C'mon," Ellen said as she took off her shoes and clasped them in her right hand, "let's hit the beach!" She took off over the planter, and in a somewhat straight line, headed for the darker beach area. It was well lit by the full moon, so he had no trouble following her. He grabbed her hand and slowed her to a walk, but she kept pulling, trying to get him to run with her. She was dodging the incoming waves. They would chase her inland a little, then she would chase them back out to sea. She pulled away from Paul and went a little too far. The next big wave tipped her over and got her wet up to her neck. She just sat there and laughed.

Paul ran to her side and reached down to pull her up. She reached up for him and, timing it perfectly, pulled him down and forward into the next wave, laughing almost uncontrollably. "Why you little...mermaid," Paul laughed. "See if I ever let you have four drinks in one night again!"

She had crawled up on the beach out of the water. He just sat down beside her when she grabbed him and pulled him down beside her, now lying on the beach. She put her hands behind his head and pulled his face toward hers. She kissed him long and hard. Her hands left his head and stroked his back. She pressed her body tight to his. "Paul, I want you. I want you so much." She kissed him again like she had never kissed before. Her body was sending him unmistakable signals. He returned her kisses, but finally got her to her feet. Arms around waists they headed for the Royal Sands.

"Can I join you?" a meek voice spoke from the next lanai. Paul looked over, then at his watch. It was 10:30 a.m. He had ordered the room service breakfast special and was enjoying it on his lanai. He was

131

about half through.

"Do you have an appointment?" He gave her a mock stern look. "I'll get the door." She appeared in her robe as he opened the adjoining door. He gave her a quick kiss on the forehead before taking her hand and leading her to his lanai.

She put her hand to her head as she shook it. "I don't feel too hot. And, if I acted the way I think I did last night, I'm going to feel worse. Did I?"

"You did," replied Paul, "but don't worry, the police won't pick you up until noon." he laughed softly.

Ellen smiled a wan smile, using her hand to shield the sun from her eyes while looking sideways at Paul through half closed eyes. "No, I mean...you and me...did I..."

"You put on a little show, true, but you were just having fun. The minute I got you to your room you passed out cold. I took your shoes from you, got you a little comfortable, covered you up and wished you a very happy evening." He put a palm on each of Ellen's cheeks and gave them a little rub. "C'mon, get dressed. Today we're going around the island to the Polynesian Cultural Center."

"This is freaky," yelled Ellen to Paul. "Is it always like this?"

"Sometimes it's windier." They had driven around the island to Kahuka point. The wind was sweeping up the rocky cliffs and driving salt spray in their faces. Turning their backs to the wind, they walked toward their car.

"Nature can sure make you feel insignificant," said Ellen. "I feel I have all the power of a mouse." They spent the afternoon browsing through the various villages of the Polynesian Cultural Center, gaining an appreciation of the friendly Polynesian cultures. The evening show was spectacular. The costumes, fire dances and the whole show was very entertaining. It was late when they got back and both agreed they should turn in right away.

Their flight to Kauai departed smoothly from runway 4 at 9:53 a.m. Sixty minutes later, they were at the car rental counter. The Moon Surf Motel and Conference Center was on a lovely beach just outside of Hanamaulu. The weather was fit for paradise. A drive up Mount Waialeale made the rest of the morning zip by. Ellen was reading a sign. "Wow, 452 inches of rainfall...in one year."

"Each year," responded Paul, "and it fills up this river." They were at the Waimea Canyon overlook. "It's like the Grand Canyon, only green."

"Spectacular," added Ellen. "Indescribable." The trip up the river to the Fern Grotto finished up the afternoon.

They had signed up for the hotel luau that evening. The breeze was light and warm as Ellen and Paul relaxed on the beach in front of their hotel, before the luau. They took turns rubbing in sunscreen and just let the time pass. The sun was setting behind a red-orange ocean of water.

The luau was great. Much food and laughter. Ellen laid off the drinks, but Paul had a few. Still at the luau, but relaxing in a chair, Paul spotted a guitar by the bar and got the okay to use it. He and Ellen separated slightly from the group and plunked down on the warm sand. Paul strummed a few chords, Ellen holding his arm in both her hands and laying her head on his shoulder. They observed the golden runway on the water as the full moon made a welcome appearance. They started to hum a couple favorites, then broke out in song. First one person joined in from the leftover luau crowd, then another, and soon a whole group of twenty or so were having a great time singing Hawaiian songs, old favorites, and fifties songs with Ellen and Paul leading the way.

Just then, Paul noticed a group of young Hawaiians headed their way carrying a guitar, ukulele and trumpet. The lead man said, "Aloha. We noticed you guys having so much fun. We're singing at the Royal Dolphin, just up the beach and we are on our half-hour break. We want to join you for one song, okay?"

"Have at it," said Paul. "What have you got in mind?"

"First, everybody grab one of these from this box. Then, you'll probably guess. It's not an island song, but I think you'll like it. Bobby, here, does a great imitation, but everybody sing!" They started up on *Sweet Caroline*. Immediately the Bic lighters were lighting up their faces and the crowd was swaying to the music. The band finished up, grabbed their equipment and, with a wave, ran back up the beach.

Finally Paul announced that *I'll Remember You* would be the last song. Someone from the crowd suggested that Paul and Ellen sing it as a duet. They politely declined, but the whole group clapped until they agreed. Paul strummed the chords. Not a word was spoken as Paul and Ellen turned from the crowd, into each other. The beautiful music of the surf played a perfect accompaniment as they sang from their heart: "I'll remember you..."

When they finished there was a full moment of silence. Then a single handclap started and soon a full blown ovation commenced. Ellen and Paul embraced, and soon were mixing among the other guests, receiving many compliments.

19

Memphis was chilled by crisp, northerly winds, making Chris pull up his collar as he walked from his hotel to the Memphis Athletic Club. He had been a member for a week now. In that time, he had become familiar with the physical layout and had even gotten a look at the old sign-in sheets. He settled into his favorite, overstuffed leather chair. It was his favorite because it was located just right – he could turn slightly one direction to be a part of most groups, or turn the other way and be excluded. Today, he was alone. He took out a panatela and lit up. He didn't like cigars, but wanted the swank image.

Squinting his eyes and looking through the smoke, Chris thought of Ellie. *I think she was going on a Hawaiian vacation sometime around now. I hope she has a good time.* They had gone to several Veteran support group meetings. Chris couldn't make every meeting as they sometimes interfered with his second job. But, he looked at her a little different now. She shocked him after the last meeting when she agreed to stop for a drink. At that time, she told him about her parents' accident, and how close she and her brother were, then how he was killed in Vietnam. He was upset that she hadn't said anything before. Plus, she was still overly upset. It was over three years ago. *Get over it girl! It happens every day.* The one good thing is he did get a nice hug from her as he tried to comfort her. But, she wasn't as strong as Chris thought. *If we're going to be together for the long haul, she's going to have to toughen up.*

Now Harlow, he thought, *there is someone tougher than she looks.* After their New Mexico trip, she had avoided him for two weeks by picking up the time cards when he was out. But, finally she showed up one day while he was there. She told Chris how it was much harder than she thought it would be. She'd spent several long evenings next to her husband's bed, thinking. Taking that life was upsetting, but every time she looked at her husband it was a stark reminder of what had been taken from her. Multiply that by 30, 40, 50 thousand families, and it became clear that something had to be done. So, she came back, fully committed. He had given her an assignment to research any politicians, in office or out, who had a major impact on the Vietnam War then, to make a list and a plan as to how to get them. She was hoping to get in on the real action. For now, he was still flying solo. She was starting to complain about that, but seemed okay yet.

Well, I'm this far, he thought. *Quite a ways from the beginnings of this plan.* He remembered when he and Harlow were sitting in the Minneapolis Public Library reading the *Memphis Journal,* trying to get background on Congressman J. T. "Ted" Tewes of the 3rd Congressional District, Memphis, Tennessee. The trip to Memphis had gone smoothly. He inquired at the athletic club and found out through a young, talkative desk clerk that J. T. "Ted" Tewes did, indeed, belong to this club, and, in fact, would be in Friday evening as usual. Seems that he would arrive late in the evening from D. C., have a 20-minute swim, hit the steam room for twenty minutes, and then, sometimes, have a massage after the club was closed. It was a privilege accorded to founding members.

Chris went to the locker room, put on swim trunks, grabbed a towel along with his athletic bag and headed for the pool. After a brief swim, he headed down the narrow hallway past the door to the whirlpool. Ten steps ahead and one to the right brought him to the steam room door. He went inside. Thursday night at 10:00 was a slow time. Nobody around. He opened his athletic bag and took out two wrenches and a 4 inch long piece of chrome pipe. He stuck his head out the door. All was quiet. He inserted a wedge between the door and door jamb, so he could work without fear of a surprise interruption. He loosened the faucet part of the steam inlet. This steam room was one where you could control the amount of steam from within the room. A temporary steam faucet was currently attached. Chris had searched many plumbing supply houses for a faucet to match the original one. He had installed the temporary one on Tuesday and brought the original to his room where he modified it. Now, he was putting the original faucet back, although slightly modified.

He checked the hall once more, saw no activity and locked himself back in the steam room. This time he installed a slightly modified thermostat as well. Then, he took out his battery-operated drill, checked the hall, and drilled four holes through the door, and then from the hall, two holes in the jamb. He plugged the fresh holes with wood putty. *Nobody will notice.* He took a whisk broom and quickly cleaned up, toweled off all traces of fingerprints, put the tools back in his bag, and went back to the locker room. *Tomorrow night, Representative J. T. Tewes...you'll pay your debt to your country.*

That same day, the waves were gently rolling in on a quiet, Kauai beach, as Hawaiian Air winged its way to Maui – the Valley Isle, Paul informed Ellen. "A mountain on each end with a valley between—like your cute little waist," he told her. Puu Kukui was to the west, and the spectacular Haleakala Crater to the east.

The airport formalities out of the way, Paul and Ellen motored towards Lahaina. "How do you like it?" asked Paul. Ellen had been quiet on the flight. He could tell she was in one of her slight *moods*, so he didn't say much.

"I'm so grateful you arranged this little trip, Paul. I haven't had such a relaxing time in years. And, I'm not that old! It's almost sinful," she laughed lightly. She slid over as close as she could get, put both hands around his biceps and laid her head on his shoulder. He responded by laying his face on her head for a couple seconds.

"Look, the quaint little fishing village. Just as advertised." They parked and browsed through the shops, enjoying the fantastic sun and warm trade winds. The shop keepers were warm and friendly, greeting them and bidding them goodbye with a cheerful *Aloha*. They felt like honored guests in each store. Ellen walked lightly and bubbled with her usual infectious enthusiasm. Each picked out souvenirs for friends back home.

Their hotel was set back off the road among palm trees, green grass, tropical plants and many shrubs. Once again, their adjoining rooms were available, per reservations. After a light dinner, they headed for the sand and coral beach. After a quick dip in the turquoise blue water, they proceeded to lotion each other up. *She looks spectacular in her new bathing suit*, thought Paul. He had seen it before, but couldn't help thinking the same thing every time he saw her in it. Their tans were progressing, but, "It takes more than 5 or 6 days in the sun to look like we belong here," Paul had to remind Ellen.

Watching the sun set into the Pacific had become a favorite time for them, so they lingered at the beach, waiting for the breathtaking show. It seemed that time stood still, and that a special feeling passed between them as they lay on their towels holding hands, while the sun sank into the water.

"It's like the end of all hurt and pain," Ellen remarked, "and the preface to an all new tomorrow, the beginning of the rest of our lives. What would you do different with your life, if you could live it over? Did you ever think about that?" She rolled onto her side, facing him.

He remained on his stomach, resting his chin on his clasped hands. He turned to look at her. "That's a good question. You know I have thought about it once in a while, but I don't know. For one thing, I can't live it over, and I'm satisfied with who I am and where I am for now. Oh sure, I plan to get better, and I have made my share of mistakes, but that's life." He smiled at her, rolled over and sat up. "And, I'll make more mistakes and do some more things right. No, I don't look back much. Today is the only day I can live, so I try to do a good job with the present, and that, little princess, is why I am here with you. It's what I most want right now."

Ellen sat up, pulled her knees up with her arms, rested her chin on her knees and stared at the golden red trail the setting sun imprinted on the surface of the Pacific. "Did you mean those words we sang together on the beach in Kauai?" She didn't look at him.

He maneuvered so he was right in front of her, lifting her chin with his hands.

"Yes, except the song implies we'll be parting, and I hope that is not the case."

Ellen took a deep breath. "This is going to sound so lame, but bear with me. You were right earlier when you said I miss Steve. Every day

I miss him a lot. I know I'll never forget him, and I know how I am handling it is not right. When I let you get too close, it's like I'm cheating on him. We're both mature enough where we could take our relationship to the next level. And, I thank you so much for being patient with me. It's my fault. You deserve more. You are so good to me. I feel right when we're together, yet when the romance gets going, I'm in one hundred percent...up to a point, whatever it is. I am so sorry. This is so lame." She paused, took another big breath and continued, "It's almost like I'm in love with who Steve was. We were so close. He would get jealous if I brought a date home; I would get jealous if he went with someone. I know it's not right, and I really am working on it. You have got to me more than anyone ever has. Please do not give up on me."

"C'mon," he said as he pulled her to her feet. "I'm not going anywhere. You'll get there when you are ready. If we get to that next level, I want it to be when you want it, not when you think you should, or when I think you should, but when you're really ready. Let's go have a drink. Happy Valentine's day!"

Chris stopped into the massage room and visited with old Billy Bob Jansy, the club masseur. He casually pried a little information from Billy Bob. Yes, J.T. the Congressman usually had a massage each Friday night, no he did not have an appointment, and yes sometimes he was too busy to stay. "Well," Chris said as he stood at the door, "I understand he has a late meeting tonight and probably won't have time, but you should stay, you know, just in case. By the way, I got a job in New Orleans, so I'll be moving on. You won't have to put up with me after Friday."

"Ah, well," Billy Bob said to the empty doorway, "I haven't got anything better to do."

Chris propped the whirlpool door open just a bit, so he could catch a glimpse of anybody walking by. It was just about closing, and, although the Congressman had the run of the place, Chris would have to be out by the 11:30 closing time. Just then, two white legs whisked by. Chris climbed out of the whirlpool and headed for the steam room. The place was almost deserted at this late hour. So far things had gone Chris' way. He entered the steam room and nodded at the guest sitting across from him pretending not to notice who he was or even to pay any attention to him.

Checking his watch, he noticed time was running out. He left the steam room without saying a word and went to the front desk. "Got a towel, John? I seem to have misplaced mine." The desk clerk obliged. "Going to lock up soon?"

"Yah, soon as you get out." Glancing at the wall clock, "We close at 11:30 ya know."

"Sure," replied Chris. "It's my last time here. I'm moving on. Got a job in New Orleans. Oh, there's still a guy down in the steam room."

"No problem. He's a big wheel. Got his own key. If I waited for him every Friday, I'd never get home."

"Yah, sure—look, he said to tell Billy Bob not to wait for him. You know what he's talking about?" The clerk nodded and headed towards Billy Bob's office. "Hey, I'm getting my clothes on and will be out in five minutes," he yelled to the departing clerk. He waited until the desk clerk was out of sight and went into the locker room. He stuffed all his clothes into his athletic bag and went down the other hall to re-enter the steam room.

141

Sitting in the steam room, he knew the timing would be close. Glancing at his watch he judged the clerk should almost be checked out and locked up. He did seem anxious to leave. He couldn't wait too long or J. T. would leave. Chris got up to leave and as he did he gave the steam room knob a quick turn. He felt the valve inside break and knew there was no way to stop the cloud of steam that was coming. *Eternal steam*, thought Chris, as he secured the door behind him, slipping a steel peg into the lock set-up he had installed earlier on the outside of the door.

He stepped into a doorway and quickly changed clothes. He had a ski mask folded up on his head to look like the stocking cap he always wore—in Memphis, anyway—just in case anybody was around. He listened carefully and could only hear muffled yelling and pounding at the steam room door. *Good thing they make those doors good and strong,* he thought, as he slipped unnoticed out the side door.

He walked four blocks to where he had left his van, hopped in and headed towards Minneapolis. He planned to stop near St. Louis around 7:00 in the morning, sleep for four or five hours, check the news, shave off his beard, get a haircut, and head for home. *Another mission accomplished.* He smiled. Something to be said for self-fulfillment, knowing you were doing your part to right some wrongs. Yes sir, it wasn't a picnic, but *somebody has to do it.* Traffic was light, and soon Memphis was a fading memory.

The Maui morning was beautiful. Ellen turned back to watch her footsteps disappear in the wet sand. She enjoyed having some early morning solitude almost any day of the year, but it was especially precious this morning. The sun hadn't been up for long, and the warm

142

tropical breeze was a welcome contrast to her memories of February mornings in Minnesota. A sense of wellbeing pervaded her entire being as she twirled down to meet the waves, then skipped just out of their reach. A flock of shore birds searched the sand for breakfast, then took flight in unison, soaring and diving, paying no attention to her. It was like she was alone in paradise; all alone. *Fun for a while*, she thought. Then looking back at their hotel, she thought of Paul. *Still sleeping, no doubt.* Then, she peered across the ocean toward where she imagined Vietnam, and Steve, to be.

Dear Paul, she mused, as she slowly made her way back to the hotel, *not pushing me, being very understanding, sharing my thoughts and feelings that I don't even understand, being funny when I need it, being serious when I want. I want to love him with all my heart, yet I can't seem to let go – to give him all of it. It's like half my heart isn't mine to give. If anyone should have my love and devotion, it certainly would be him.*

She was nearing the hotel and broke into a run. Up in her room, she grabbed her bathrobe and called Paul's room. She heard his phone ringing and soon a sleepy voice said, "Hello?"

"Hey, sleepy head. Wake up! You're missing the best part of the day."

"Get lost. I hate people who are cheerful at," a pause, "6:30 in the morning! Just a minute…your door open?" A minute later, Paul entered her room with just a bathing suit on. "C'mon, we're going swimming!"

"I was just down there!" she said as she stood on her tip toes and gave him a quick kiss on the lips, "but I'm ready to go again."

The beach was great and the time passed quickly. Soon, they were headed to the airport to catch the noon flight to the Big Island of

Hawaii.

It was on the front page of section B of the *Kansas City Republican*: "Tennessee Congressman Dead in Gruesome Mishap." As the waitress refilled his coffee cup, Chris read on. Nothing in the story said that the police connected this "accident" with the previous executions, but then Chris knew the police didn't tell the reporters everything. In a day or two, the reporters would piece it together and publish their own theories. That would give his cause the publicity it deserved. He smiled as he thought of the Congressmen who would be looking over their shoulders wondering when it was their turn. Now maybe they'd have a little sense of what the people they sent out on useless patrols in a useless war felt like. *Sweat, you suckers, sweat!*

"Indescribable."

"Yes, awesome." Paul turned to Ellen and smiled. "I mean how would you describe this scene in words?" After landing in Hilo, they had started their afternoon sightseeing with a trip to Akaka Falls. He put his arm around her waist as they balanced on a rock watching the thin blue string of water plunge 420 feet into a white frothy pool all framed by lush, green vegetation. Next, it was back to Hilo for a quick dinner and drink.

The next morning, they started touring with a trip to Mauna Kea, Hawaii's highest point. Paul made sure they had sweaters along. Ellen couldn't believe how cold it was as they hiked the visitor's trail near the summit.

The pool at the hotel was inviting, and they took a quick dip before dinner. Tomorrow they would pack up and head to Kona on the west side of the island. The evening was pleasant. They took in an early show, sat and talked for a while, and decided to get a good night's rest. As great as it was, vacationing was proving to be more work than they thought.

The next day flew by, marred only by a brief afternoon downpour. Otherwise Hawaii delivered on its promise of a tropical paradise. They finally returned to their original hotel in Honolulu six days after leaving it. Tomorrow would be the long flight back to Minneapolis, but first, Paul announced, "One more evening of dining, dancing, and frivolity. And, you may have two Mai-Tais."

Ellen laughingly agreed as they parted to their respective hotel rooms. Paul took a nap and was startled awake by his phone. "Hey, you passed out or something? I knocked on your door till my hand swelled up!"

"No, no," replied Paul still groggy. "I fell asleep and now I feel like a truck ran over me." Glancing at his watch he said, "Give me half an hour, and I'll pick you up for our aloha dinner, okay?"

Half an hour later, Ellen opened her door to Paul's knock and saw the surprised look on his face. She had secretly bought a new outfit for this special night. A pure white, coarse silk-looking dress with tiny wisps of gold colored thread throughout. It tied over one shoulder, plunged somewhat provocatively and closed under the other arm exposing a bare shoulder. She knew she was overdressed for Hawaii, but didn't care. Paul's date was going to be the best looking woman in Honolulu tonight. He deserved it. The white dress contrasted beautifully with her nicely tanned body.

"Ellen, I—I had no idea. Why you look simply...ravishing! Let's just stay here tonight." Paul said quickly, as he jokingly pulled her back into her room.

"Hold on there, Tiger." Ellen said throatily, "Let's go eat."

Paul was conscious of almost every head turning and appraising Ellen as the hostess led them to their reserved table. The dinner show was an exceptionally well-done dance and play depicting the early history of Hawaii. Afterwards they slipped into the lounge, featuring a trio of Hawaiian singers with a small band, and a dance floor.

Dancing close together, cheek to cheek, Ellen felt very warm, and protected. As they danced, Ellen said, "Paul, it seems to me like we've been here half my life. I mean I can't hardly remember Minneapolis, or my job, or my apartment. It's crazy." Ellen spoke softly as she followed Paul around the dance floor, "It's also fantastic!"

"Total immersion," Paul said. "When you're really caught up in something and give it your full attention, it becomes a big part of yourself, almost to the exclusion of everything else. I'm glad to see you enjoying yourself. I was really pleased when you said you would come along. I imagine there will be some *talk* when you get home again."

"Oh, I suppose. But, I'm a big girl, remember? I can decide for myself what I want to do. There is nobody really close for me since..." her voice trailed off as she realized she hadn't thought of Steve for a day now. It made her feel guilty. She continued, "since Steve and now, you." She sagged noticeably, and clung to Paul, her body becoming less tense. They walked back to their table silently, and finished their drinks. Ellen spoke first, "Let's take a walk on the beach?" she suggested. Paul nodded, and stepped over to her chair, pulling it back as she got up.

He whispered in her ear, "You are the most beautiful girl in Hawaii tonight." She smiled a hesitant smile at him as they headed for the beach.

By 10:30 p.m., all the beach crowds were gone. They passed a couple small groups here and there – a solitary person or two. Songs and ukulele music drifted to them from the various hotel terraces. The constant music of the Pacific surf was like an ever present symphony. Hand in hand they walked, saying nothing, feeling everything. Ellen stopped and turned toward Paul. She put her arms around his waist and invited his kiss. Paul reached down and pulled Ellen to him. Kissing her hard on the lips, tasting the salt from the tears flowing down her cheeks.

She sagged down to the sand. Paul sat beside her. Her face was silhouetted between him and the moon. Her cheeks glistened and her dress reflected the lunar rays. *She looks like a goddess*, Paul thought.

Ellen spoke, "Isn't it sad? It's almost over. I don't want this to end. I don't want to go back."

He put his arm around her shoulder. She snuggled closer to him. "They tell me a lot of people feel that way after being here, but...."

"I know," Ellen interrupted, "that we have to go back. And, I'll be on that plane tomorrow, but, you know what I mean." She turned toward him with her beautiful smile in place again.

"Yes, I know." Paul looked away, eyes focusing 1,000 miles out into the ocean, "We've got our work calling us." He thought about some of the work she didn't know about. *If she knew of some of my plans, she might not be sitting here beside me.*

Ellen had turned slightly away from him to gaze at the infinite waves pounding the beach. Incessant. Wild. Never ending. Alpha and Omega. Before man, and after man. Every wave different, but essentially the same. Paul's thoughts returned to the present as he observed Ellen. He noticed again how beautiful she was. And, for the first time, he really wanted her. His stomach started churning as he contemplated his dilemma. He would never violate the trust she had shown him. If only she would show the slightest willingness, he would not hesitate to spend this, their last night in Hawaii, in her bed. After all, he was an adult, she was an adult, and tonight she was sober.

"C'mon," she said, breaking his thoughts, "we better head to the hotel. We've got a big day tomorrow. Okay, ol' Chap?"

They walked slowly, arms around waists, kicking sand and talking about the things they had seen and done. At her hotel room door Ellen hesitated a second, then invited Paul in. He called room service right away and ordered champagne. It was soon delivered, and they sat out on her lanai enjoying the tropical breezes that blew lightly, but firmly, across the lanai. You could tell neither one really wanted to give in to the reality of time. The conversation was light and melancholy. After a while, Paul got up to leave. He took Ellen's hand as they walked to the door between their rooms. Paul reached for Ellen's waist and pulled her close. She offered no resistance and sensed a difference in Paul's demeanor. He seemed more insistent, more demanding. She gave herself fully to him as they kissed hotly and frantically.

Suddenly she pulled away. He let her go. She put her arms around him and gave him a big hug. "Well, I'll see you in the morning," said Paul. "Breakfast at 7:00 sharp. See you." Paul left abruptly and shut the door harder than he intended.

He had no hard feelings and could certainly respect Ellen's feelings. *Someday!* He sat on the edge of his bed and thought why did he get mixed up with a girl who was living in the past half the time. *Well, not quite half the time, but she was certainly dragging a big anchor. But, she is so special! But, then I guess if I had been orphaned, depending on my big brother like she had to, I might see things differently. Maybe*

I would feel the same way. I've got to give her some more time. And, maybe if I do my secret job properly no other families will have to go through what war does to them. Paul got up, shut his light off and quietly slipped into the hall. A walk on the beach alone would feel good, he couldn't sleep anyway.

After Paul left her room, Ellen aimlessly walked out on the lanai and sat down. She had never seen Paul quite this way. He was always so even tempered and in control. Actually, it was rather exciting. Paul had lost a little of his control, and she had caused it. She always felt a barrier between them, not big, but it was there. Now it seemed to be crumbling, Paul was more human, less perfect. More hers. She looked up at the stars, shook her head and started humming. A smile on her face, she went back into her room, took a quick shower, put on her short little nightie, dabbed perfume in the usual spots, and dialed Paul's room.

She could hear the phone ringing. No answer. She laid down on her bed with a big smile. He's probably in the shower, she thought. As she laid there she closed her eyes, relaxed, and brought up an image of Paul singing to her like she was the only girl in the whole world. She tried again at 12:15, then at 12:30, again at 12:45. By 1:00 she was sleeping.

20

"Paul, I have good news and bad news," Ellen said breathlessly as she greeted Paul with a peck on the cheek, at their favorite restaurant back home.

"Should I be worried?" queried Paul. "But wait, let's order a bottle of wine first," he said while waving the waiter down. After returning from Hawaii, they both had to double down at work to make up for being gone, plus their businesses were getting busier. Spring was when a lot of the firm's building projects got started, and it was important to oversee the foundation work, placement on the property and the inevitable sub-contractor problems.

For Ellen, Easter season was very busy at the store. Her clientele always wanted to look new and fresh in the first warm days of spring. So, since returning from paradise, besides phone calls and coffee, they had only been able to find time for two real dates.

"Paul, it is so good to see you again – we are both so darn busy. I miss you."

"I don't know how it can be two months already since we got back. Every day I think of you—sometimes even twice a day! Especially in that bikini," he chuckled.

The wine came and they talked about work, wanting to catch up on all the happenings of each other's daily lives.

As Paul refilled their glasses, Ellen scrunched up her face and looked at Paul. "What is that look for?" he asked.

"A couple things. First, I've toyed with the idea of being a coach/chaperone for my old touring group—The All-American Touring Chorus—for the last couple years. I know the director, and she always asks me. It's four months in Japan and Europe: June 15th to September 15th. Also, at work, Mrs. Thoms wants me to take on more responsibility along with a nice raise. If I do that, and I plan to, it means I will never have a chance to tour with the chorus. I could never take four months off."

"Hold that thought," said Paul as the waiter came to take their order. "I know what I want. How 'bout you, Ellen?"

"I'm having my favorite. Go ahead and order it for me. I'll see if you remember."

"Of course," he replied, slyly. Paul placed their orders, remembering exactly what she wanted. "Now, you were saying?"

"I was saying...but sitting here across from you," she took both his hands in hers, "it doesn't sound as appealing as it did an hour ago. I was about to say, Mrs. Thoms' sister in New York is retiring. Well, as Mrs. Thoms described the new responsibilities, I did tell her I would do it and how grateful I was that she has faith in me. I also told her that not being able to do the European/Japanese tour would be a bit of a disappointment. She told me her sister would be glad to have an excuse to spend some time with her in Minneapolis, and she could fill in for me if I wanted to go on this one, last, long adventure. The time to go would be now, before the new duties consume my time."

"So, are you going?" Paul looked pensive over the top of his wine glass.

"Oh, Paul, I know I should have talked to you first, but I also knew I had to go. I hope you understand."

Paul looked off to the side, put his wine glass on the table and twirled it by the stem with both hands, looked back at Ellen, put one hand on his forehead and wiped down over his face.

Ellen knew he would be frustrated, at least she hoped he would be. Considering that it meant time away from him, she was too.

"Ellen," he took her hands, "you know I want you to be happy. It sounds like an important opportunity. I'm happy for you. I would rather have you to myself, but I guess I can share you with the world. I will miss you, a lot."

"Thank you. It wasn't an easy decision, and you are the reason it wasn't an easy one. I shouldn't even mention this, because the chances of anything big happening are quite small, but, by going back to Japan, and meeting with my mentors there, if I can find them, I may get some help in dealing with the loss of my brother." With that she paused and took a couple breaths. "I'm sorry I'll be gone so long. Paul, you know I love you, and I know our relationship may not be all you would want, so, I don't know, so...if you want, if...you feel like you—ah, might want to, ah, date others, I can understand." With that she put her hand up to cover her mouth as her eyes started to water.

The waiter was just bringing the food as Paul stood up to take Ellen by the hand. "Go ahead," he told the waiter, "we'll be right back." He led Ellen to a mostly secluded area just off the lobby, encircled her waist and pulled her into a tight embrace. "Ellen, I've been in the war. I saw the devastation in the troops. I also know that it's not just the soldiers that suffer, but all those close to them. We are doing just fine. I will wait for you. Just you. C'mon."

After dinner, Paul had to stop by his office to get a few things ready for an early-morning meeting, so they had driven separately to the restaurant. Alone, and on her way home, Ellen thought about telling Chris about her upcoming absence. She had been avoiding him lately. *He seems to have turned dark, in a way, plus he's always going out of town for seminars or business trips.* She decided to let it go.

21

Chris checked his black bow tie in the dirty, round mirror, adjusted it a little to the right, ran his hand along his slicked black hair, checked the shine on his shoes, and headed for the motel room door. Pausing at the desk right before the door, he slipped on a black coverall, wire rim glasses, a fake beard, and a black bowler hat. Up close this would fool no one, but from a distance he looked like a Mennonite. It was just for anybody who might see him leave his motel room. When he got near the college, it would all come off, and he would be back in his college maintenance man outfit.

He and Harlow had put this plan together in his St. Paul apartment, and it was time to carry it out down in Omaha where he was now. Actually, he was headed to John Amery College to "work," though he did not have a real job there.

First, though, Chris swung into the rear parking lot of the All Roads Shopping Center. It was practically deserted, as usual. Climbing into the back of his van he removed his coveralls, glasses and beard, leaving his maintenance man disguise intact. Checking for curious onlookers out the side window and finding none, Chris climbed out of his van, locked it, strode to the east parking lot, and unlocked his old car. He bought it from an old farmer who asked no questions after seeing cash.

Senator Tom Stout of Nebraska was going to speak at the 5th Annual John Amery Countryside Assembly, at the college, exactly one week

154

from today. *It was time to step up execution of his plan*, thought Chris, execution being a good word choice. *It sure is.*

Heading for the college, Chris recalled how pleased he was to finally find an event happening in Senator Stout's hometown. He was one of the biggest hypocrites of the war. Stout was one of the first to demand that our troops be sent to Vietnam, then when popular opinion soured, he made a big plea for limiting the kinds of armaments and hardware that could be used there. Fortunately his views did not prevail entirely, but between that and Stout's convenient turnabout on any military involvement, he was one of Chris' top ten.

Chris and Harlow regularly read about ten newspapers at the public library, and she noticed a small announcement in the Omaha paper about his impending visit to John Amery College in June. Then, they started planning.

Chris parked on the street right next to the employee parking area. He had no official parking sticker, but wanted it to appear he was parking in the lot, so he exited his car at opportune times, and walked through the lot as if he had parked there. He entered the college through the employee entrance and walked purposely down the hall. He would prefer not to meet any maintenance people, but was carrying a gas leak detector and could use that for cover. Nobody, except a few of the maintenance people, would even question him.

Today, he needed to get into the commons room, where, in one week, the good Senator and about 200 university officials, community leaders and selected students would have lunch prior to his 1:30 speech. Finding the room empty, Chris entered and looked around. He needed three chairs but didn't want to draw attention to himself. He found a rolling chair carrier with about 20 chairs on it. Thinking it would be more common to roll the whole carrier than pick three chairs, he started tugging and finally got the rack moving. He had just entered the hall when a regular maintenance man came around the corner and into his hall.

"Watcha doin?" he rasped.

"Well I, ah, I'm supposed to move these chairs down the hall," Chris kept his voice even and added a little whine to it. "I don't know why and they don't give me no help. Did they send you?"

"You kiddin'? I got the gym to finish up, then I'm supposed to help Orv with the track. Got a track meet tomorrow, course you guys over here in Student Center land don't know nothin' about that. Besides, you're new. I didn't know Student Center was gettin' another man. When did you start?"

"Oh, I'm just a temp. Guess they needed some extra help because of some big luncheon next week. I mainly work in the administrative area. Well, gotta get rollin', see ya."

The man seemed satisfied as Chris pushed and got the cart rolling again. At the end of the hall, he grabbed three chairs and went through the employee lot. He could always claim he was taking them to the repair shop if he got stopped. He wasn't. When no one was looking he skipped out of the lot over to his car.

Back at the shopping center parking lot, he transferred the chairs to his van, locked his car in this apparently safe place, put his disguise back on, and headed for his motel. Dinner was burger and fries to-go from the Quick-Stop drive in. Then it was time to work on the chairs.

He soon tired of working on the chairs and gazed out his window. He noticed the night clerk drive into work in an old battered car and got an idea. He stopped in the office when he could see there were no customers. There weren't many anyway, as the place was a bit run down. After visiting with the clerk, turns out he needed a different car. They agreed on a price to be paid Friday if the car was all Chris said it was. He would bring it around tomorrow for the clerk to look at. He made up some story about moving to New Orleans and not needing two cars anymore. The car wasn't all that great, but it was better than what the clerk was driving now, and in truth, Chris just wanted to get rid of it so it wouldn't be left behind after the "accident" at the college.

Back in his room, he took out a tape recorder. He had taped a message, while home in St. Paul, on this variable speed recorder. He was now playing it and adjusting the speed slower to get a deep, bass-sounding voice. Then, he recorded the drawn-out message on another recorder. He played it again: "Ladies and gentlemen," the voice was deep and deliberate, just as he wanted it. A pause... "Ladies and gentlemen," *yes, just the right sound of urgency.* "Please do not panic. Do not move. Remain standing. Do as I say and you will not be hurt. You are under observation at this time. Do not move!" Pause... "Thank you. Senator Stout, as you know, is our guest of honor. Did you know our guest of honor is responsible for several thousand deaths? Ask him about Vietnam. Ask him!" The voice was almost shouting. "Now, easy everybody, just sit down and do not move for five minutes. If you do this, we will be gone. Enjoy your lunch. I said, sit down!" That was the end.

Chris was concerned about the length. Would they try to hustle the Senator out of there, or would the smokescreen hold? This would be the first time the true message would be heard before an execution. His letter to the *Washington Post* had caused quite a discussion. This would add to that. It could be the start of a massive national uprising against

157

those responsible for the Vietnam mess. And, if his plan didn't work, he would just try again.

The speaker that was hooked to the tape player was chosen because it sounded like a bullhorn. He had already located a closet at the side of the commons room. It had a shelf inside and a louvered door. The batteries for both the timer and cassette player were fresh. This part of the plan was all set.

Lying back on his bed after the 10:00 news, Chris clasped his hands behind his head. *I wonder what Ellie is doing tonight. I would love to give her a call, but can't risk anybody knowing where I am. Hopefully we can get together next week.*

Senator Stout and all those like him, thought Chris, *actual murderers of thousands of American young people, sending me and my generation to a useless, no-win war like it was a game. You go and kill and be killed while we figure out a way to save face. What a joke! How utterly immoral! They ought to be brought to trial like the Nazi war criminals were. But no! All they do is make money and more money. And, then they send more young men up for cannon fodder.*

Chris smiled. *Justice is being served. Some folks are pretty nervous now that three of their partners in crime have paid their dues, along with an innocent young man. This execution will work out just great,* Chris thought. *It will be in front of quite a few students, and they will appreciate what I am doing more than most. Looking good.*

He recalled his last tryst with Harlow. She was getting more and more impatient to join him. Omaha is not that far. It's a perfect time for me to come along, she pointed out. Not yet, he'd said, but he finally told her that he was down to the last three targets he had researched and planned for. Senator Stout of Nebraska, Senator Cambridge of

Michigan, and Senator Ruskins of Ohio. They were among the top ten. After them, they would work together on a new top ten list. She would be in the field with him. *Good or bad? Not sure*, he thought. One thing they had done together was go to the shooting range a couple times. He found out she was a better shot than he was!

The week went by with Chris staying mostly in his room, being noticed as little as possible. He used his disguise whenever he left the motel room, meeting as few people as possible. He went back to the college twice just to be seen briefly and to recheck the layout. One day another large luncheon was scheduled in the room, so he walked in and quickly checked the thermostat, observing the layout of the head table.

The chairs were now complete. Two chairs were dummies. They all three looked the same, but only one was lethal, and it worked great. He had set a watermelon on that one, before installing the bolts, and saw it speared right up the middle of the melon. Next he put in the bolts that would shear off under 150 pounds of pressure. Since the Senator weighed north of 200 pounds, there would be no problem. The stainless steel spike that grew upward out of an X brace connecting the bottom of the four legs looked like a part of the chair design common to those used at the head table. The sharp needle-like point was covered by a stainless steel sleeve that would drop down with under fifty pounds of pressure. Even the explosive device hidden in the back of the chair's padding was no problem. Maybe, just maybe, for a brief instant, Senator Stout would know what it would be like to be hit with a claymore mine.

The morning broke clear and still. A friendly, high-pressure system guarded the blue skies and gave the morning air a crisp, snappy feeling.

Chris knew from experience the day would turn hot and muggy. But now, at 6:00 a.m., it was beautiful.

Senator Stout was enjoying the same morning from his Omaha home about twenty miles away. But, not enjoying the morning as much as he might. He had not enjoyed life quite as much since reading Bob Benson's column in the Washington paper about six months ago. Benson speculated about the "Nam" killings, as he called them. Benson had researched the original stances and then the changes of political rhetoric by the first three Congressmen killed, and then drew a list of seven more who had similar patterns. Senator Stout's name made the list. So had J. T. "Ted" Tewes, who had died in that horrible steam room incident. The casket had been closed at the funeral, but rumor had it that his skin had peeled off like an onion.

Ever since that article, Stout had a premonition of a terrible accident. This was especially true the further he got from Washington. Of course these premonitions were most likely false, but still, they took a toll on Stout. His friends noticed him growing thinner and paler. His aide had even booked him into the Mayo Clinic next week on Tuesday.

Stout had taken quite a while to shake the Vietnam stigma. It was easy to jump on the bandwagon with Johnson and McNamara early on. The war was popular, and the voters demanded it. After all, this war couldn't last long – the mighty United States against a puny little bunch of Viet Cong. But slowly, at first, the tide turned. McNamara was promising to bring our boys home soon, but they didn't come home, except in body bags. To make matters worse, we weren't close to winning the war. There was no end in sight. The public smelled a rat, and the war soon became an unpopular cause. It was politically expedient to change positions. Stout did. He felt some guilt at first, but

160

with elections coming up he began speaking as vigorously against the war, as he had for it earlier. He thought he had made it through the 180 degree opinion shift, but wasn't quite so sure now.

Chris arrived at 7:00 a.m. He knew the regular maintenance men took care of another building until 9:30; then they would come to the commons to set up for the luncheon. He intended to have the head table set up by then. The day staff would attribute the setting up to the late shift, so that would work out. Like with any of these executions, if it didn't work out, he would be gone and try again another day.

He went down to get the chair cart so as not to draw attention to the three altered chairs. The head table chairs were a lot fancier than the run-of-the-mills, but they were still hauled on the same cart. All went well as he set up the head table. He had a "safety bolt" on the lethal chair and knew he would have to risk coming back closer to noon when the other tables were set and the name tents were placed, to remove it. He would also have to discreetly set the timer on the tape player and on the chair.

Chris waited patiently in his car until he saw the Senator's motorcade coming, if you could call two cars a motorcade. He then headed to the commons room carrying his gas detector with him. The room was bustling with activity as pink uniformed ladies were busy setting the salads and wicker baskets of buns wrapped in checkered cloth.

He has guessed correctly about the Senator's place, and had no trouble knocking the safety bolt out, and setting the chair timer as he pretended to make last minute adjustments. The two dummy chairs on either side made all three look like normal, head-table chairs. Chris slipped unnoticed among the bustle, into the closet, and set the tape recorder timer to ten minutes, shut the door and slipped into the hall. He knew it would be close, but these meetings were run very efficiently at John Amery College.

As the Senator's group arrived in the hall, Chris ducked into a nearby restroom. He wanted to be very low profile. He looked at his watch. Nine minutes, ten seconds. Slipped back into the hall behind the Senator. The Senator stopped in the commons room doorway to greet some people and visited with them for about three minutes. The Senator strode directly to his chair. Chris re-entered the room with a folding chair under each arm and was pretending to be busy, while really watching the senator. "Not yet," Chris whispered as the Senator was about to sit in his chair.

"Senator, Senator Stout – would you stand by the Mayor for a quick picture? That's it. Great, thanks for your time." The local photographer was doing her job. The picture taking was complete. Ten seconds to go.

"Ladies and gentlemen," the voice boomed through the loudspeaker from the direction of the closet, people were milling around, the Senator was close to his seat. The voice continued with the recorded message, the crowd hushed in no time and though confused, listened closely, not knowing what to do. At the mention of the Senator's Vietnam flip flop, he turned bright red as all the eyes of the crowd were on him. As the message concluded, the people went obediently to their seats.

Chris' eyes were hard on the Senator. It was almost like slow motion. The Senator sat down, there was a little jerk to his head, and his body slowly settled downward. Chris could see the look of helplessness on his face, a look of bewilderment and pain. Suddenly, as the Senator slid closer to the floor, a high-pitched wail emerged from his red lips. It changed quickly to a gurgle, with blood frothing at the mouth and being sprayed outward in droplets propelled by the last out rush of air from a ruptured diaphragm and lungs. Chris could picture the giant stainless steel spike violating the Senator's body.

Slowly the Senator settled to the floor, the chair tipped backwards as designed, further impaling the Senator on four miniature spikes embedded in the back of the chair. Just then, the small explosive charge hidden in the chair back went off, lifting the Senator about five feet in the air, freeing his tortured body from its momentary captivity.

Chris was running down the hall heading for his car yelling, "Ambulance, call an ambulance!" He left the car and keys at the motel as previously arranged with the clerk, and walked the three miles to his van. Soon, he was on roads that would lead him home. To Ellie, and Harlow.

This may be the start of a national drive to rid the world of these murderers once and for all, thought Chris, a purifying task that had to be done. He could soon be the new national hero. And, *a deserving one*.

22

"Maybe yes, maybe no." Chris was talking to himself in his van. The night was crisp, clear and downright cold. The streets were slippery with hard packed icy snow, so Chris had to force more concentration on his driving and less on his apparent problem with Ellie. They had dated occasionally for over two years now, and he had not been able to get close to her. More like she was tolerating him, or forcing herself to spend time with him. He had not pushed it either, Chris reflected, but then he had not been encouraged either. It was all so confusing. Yet, Ellie seemed like his property. He knew she didn't want to be "owned," but he couldn't help it. She had lost her parents in a car accident and her brother in the war, so she had no family. She needed protecting. Like a benevolent dictator, he would protect her.

That's why he was chasing around west Minneapolis trailing Ellie. If she was seeing another man, it was about time he stepped in and did some protecting. She said about a year ago she had found someone she really liked, and ever since then their dates were more like quick meetings over coffee, or a little time together at the support group meetings. And now, she had started to find excuses to even avoid that. Maybe she was seeing too much of one man.

"Now where did she go?" murmured Chris. He had lost her! He started driving in ever-widening circles of blocks and was about to give up when he saw her hand over her Mustang keys to the valet in front of the Normandie, a quaint little French restaurant in west Minneapolis. Just behind her, a big black Buick pulled up and honked. Ellie turned back and walked to the open passenger side window, stuck her head in the car for a few seconds, turned and went through the restaurant's front door. The Buick then headed for the back parking lot as Chris waited for the driver to return. Just then, two cabs pulled up behind Chris, and one honked impatiently for him to unblock the street. He pulled forward and had his view of the Normandie entrance and parking lot blocked by an old Tudor house just as he glimpsed a tall, young man enter. He went around the block and back to the parking lot.

"Hey! What took you so long—slow poke?" Ellen joked. "I almost got picked up twice." They had agreed to meet here, and Paul couldn't believe the timing. Both arriving within the same minute. Paul didn't trust his car to any valet, so had parked it himself in the back parking lot. Paul removed his coat and took both theirs to the coat room. He enjoyed this restaurant and he enjoyed Ellen's company. After seeing each other only once a week, or so, for the past months, they had been getting together two or three times a week lately, as their schedules lightened up. *I like it this way*, thought Paul. Right after Ellen got back from the All-American Touring Chorus trip, Mrs. Thoms had gotten quite ill, so Ellen had to take over her duties and worked pretty much night and day. Paul also had gotten extra busy at work with his usual projects and some unexpected clients.

Ellen seemed to come alive when she was with Paul. "I feel—um, put together, whole, I feel good, when I'm with Paul," Ellen told Karen, one of the few store managers her own age, and one of her few good friends. I haven't felt quite like this since...Steve."

They moved to their favorite table in front of the blazing fireplace and ordered their usual wine and meal from a surprisingly vivacious older waitress. "Ellen, you look absolutely stunning. You glow, you sparkle, you bring out the poet in me. You are, uhm...magic!"

"What do you think that little speech will get you?" Ellen laughed lightly as she took her wine glass at the rim with both hands. Then quietly, seriously, she said, "Thank you, Paul, you are very nice."

The slight feeling of inadequacy gnawed at her thoughts, but was dismissed. Paul meant it. He was sincere. He wasn't trying to be European about it. After knowing him for two years, she knew it was him – genuine Paul Grayson, special limited edition.

Outside, the air was freezing, but even so, the figure that had been under the black Buick with a pair of snippers had no gloves on. His breath left momentary clouds of ice crystals as he ran across the parking lot, around the corner, and entered his van. Hands were rubbed together, gloves reestablished, ignition sparked the engine to come to life, and one more vehicle entered a main artery into the city, through it, and on to the next city: St. Paul.

Inside the Normandie, the warmth of the fireplace, the amber glow of the dimmed French chandeliers, and the after dinner French wine made for a nostalgic conversational setting. Paul and Ellen were enjoying recapping the last two years and treading lightly into the future.

"Ellen, do you mind? The wine must be going to my head. I feel fairly dizzy all of the sudden. Actually, it's probably that blasted Asian flu bug. Half of the office has had it over these last two weeks. I suppose it's my turn. Hey, I'm sorry about this Ellen."

Ellen's hands reached across the small table and covered Paul's.

"Just sit back. You can't help it. Take it easy. I hope it's nothing serious."

"No, it's probably one of those two-day deals. People tell me it hits hard and fast, and then in two days you're back to normal...if you take care of yourself. Wow!" Paul grabbed at the chair with one hand and steadied himself with the other on the table as he tried to stand. "This is no good. Ellen, maybe you could get my car for me and bring it to the front door. I better get home and weather this thing out. This is quite embarrassing you know." He tried a small smile as he sat back down.

"Yes, good idea," agreed Ellen, as she went around to Paul's side to help him into his chair. She could feel how warm he was and that sweat had already soaked through his shirt. "Maybe we should take you to the hospital." She hoped he would take hold of the idea with her gentle suggestion.

"Ha, ha, just what I need. No, just bring the car around. Here's the keys. In fact, would you drive me home? I don't think I dare ride in yours feeling like this. Then take my car home and we'll get yours tomorrow. I'm going to the restroom and should be back at our table by the time you get here. Just come in and get me. I'll be okay."

Ellen took her coat from the coat room and glanced back at a sagging, pale looking Paul as she went out into the quiet, frigid night. The sidewalk was well lit, but as she turned into the parking lot it was a lot darker. A shiver ran up her spine.

Well, it's darn cold out here, she thought. *Being back in Hawaii sounds pretty good right about now.* The car was at the far end of the lot. She remembered Paul always used the rear entrance when they left. She tried several keys before dropping the whole bunch into the snow. A couple had just locked their car, nearby. The man offered to help, so

Ellen stepped behind him as he finally succeeded opening the door. He pushed the door handle's button just as a loud bang rang out from a nearby car backfiring. Ellen nearly jumped a foot, gave an apologetic laugh, thanked the man, got in, and started the car just as another backfire occurred. Startled again, she mumbled, "Enough, enough, already."

Things can turn around fast, thought Ellen. *A fantastic evening and now a sick man, me jumpy like somebody's shooting at me, a big car I'm not familiar with, and now flakes of snow on top of this ice.* She stopped at the rear parking lot exit to look for traffic, saw two young men across the street and automatically searched for the door lock button. When she looked back up, she noticed a movement off to the side with her left eye. Turning to the side window, she found herself looking directly into a bearded face with bloodshot eyes and a large scar from the bridge of his nose, going below his rheumy eye, and ending on his right cheek. She almost screamed, then realized her car had been blocking the sidewalk and the man just wanted her to move along.

With an apologetic wave, she hit the gas a little hard, swinging the back end around a little, but was finally on her way. She had to go down the little hill for two blocks, she remembered, stop at Isle Curve Boulevard, a busy street, then take a right and another right to get back to the front of the Normandie.

Heading down the hill was a little hazardous, so Ellen lightly tapped the brakes. Nothing. She stepped on them a little harder. Still nothing. The big black car was gaining speed as she frantically pumped the brakes. Isle Curve Boulevard was rapidly approaching, and Ellen could see four lanes of busy traffic ahead of her. "God, what do I do?" she cried out. "The emergency brake! Where is it?" she screamed. The speedometer registered 40 miles per hour as the front end of the big black car just missed the tail end of a brand new, yellow Cadillac. The Kenworth behind the Cadillac could do nothing but plow into the rear of the Buick, spinning it around so that the trailing gravel truck could hit it head on and push it another good 30 yards before it came to a grinding halt.

As Paul waited for Ellen's return with his arms crossed on the table and head down, he heard the ambulance and police sirens, but thought nothing of them. They were, of course, a common occurrence in the life of a city.

23

FEBRUARY 12, 1975
HOSPITAL

The icy sidewalk gave way to firmer footing as Paul neared the Steak Palace. Another meeting with Chris in an out-of-the-way meeting place. Turning his gray overcoat collar up, he faced into the wind and walked the final half block to the restaurant. Once inside, he quickly located Chris at a corner table. He gave a look around, and upon seeing Chris nod in the affirmative, headed for the table.

"Got a cup a' coffee coming for you, Cap'n. Want something to eat?"

"No, coffee's fine," said Paul, rubbing his hands together. "Well, let's get to it." Paul found himself liking to be around Chris less and less. It was nothing overt, just a feeling. Chris seemed like he was almost possessed some of the time. But then, he wasn't the only one who had a hard time adjusting. Statistics had shown that Vietnam vets had higher divorce rates, suicide rates, crime rates, and unemployment and homelessness rates than the average. It re-enforced Paul's desire to hurry up and get on with their plan. "Chris, we've been at this about two years now. We've come a long way in a short time. We've got two banks completed, two more started and six on the drawing board. It wasn't easy, but we've got one design flaw built into the banks just waiting for when we want to open the vaults."

Chris nodded. "You're right about it not being easy. I still think one of my foremen is suspicious, although when you came along and inspected the job it kinda reassured him. You know, I've been thinking, if we open these banks one at a time, how long before the FBI detects a pattern? After the second? After the third?"

"Good point," interrupted Paul. "Remember, this is a five-year plan so we've got time to work out the details—only," Paul hesitated a moment as he looked into Chris' brown eyes, "only—what would you say if we moved the schedule up a bit, say to next fall – about a year and a half from now?"

Chris looked down at his coffee which was giving up lazy swirls of steam. He had allowed the full five years for disposing of the offending, cancerous Congressmen. *I am getting better with practice*, though, he thought, *so why not?* "If you can work out the logistics, let's get started."

"Yeah, I think I can. In fact if we have six banks to open, that's about all we can handle. Your remark about leaving a pattern is true. What about this: we open three one night, and about a month later, open another three in one night, then we stop." The restaurant was not crowded so Paul didn't mind staying. It was a good place to talk, and had another hour to kill anyway before he could go up to Methodist Hospital to see Ellen.

There was an awkward silence for about thirty seconds, then Chris said, "You got it figured, then, how we're going to do three banks in one night?"

"Yes, basically we need three sets of everything each night. We pre-place a set on each bank roof, including explosives. We get in and get out—dump everything in the hole and set off another explosion. We'll want to pretty much level the place so they can't determine how we got in."

Chris seemed satisfied, at least he said nothing. "This money," Chris said, "you still got the same plans for it, too?"

"Unless you've got a better idea. I still think a national vets hotline, and a vet's newsletter to help get some political clout, and whatever other help we can come up with. We'll need a fundraising arm – not just so we can raise some additional money, but so we can funnel our proceeds into a legitimate-looking effort. I know we can reach out and help some people that the Veterans Administration is missing. What do you think?"

"Sounds good," replied Chris, thinking that what he had already done was worth more than all the political talk for the next hundred years. "Except we have to do at least two banks neither one of us had anything to do with. More would be better. Even that still would leave a pretty good pattern. We wouldn't get anything from the decoy banks, just blow them to kingdom come."

"Yes," Paul said, "that is a big weak point in our plan. Let's both give that some thought." Chris glanced at his watch. "Going somewhere?" asked Paul.

"Yeah, stopping at the hospital on the way home. Visiting hours don't start for another 45 minutes, so no hurry."

"Me too," said Paul absently. He slid his feet under the table and leaned back with his hands laced together behind his head. The clandestine work was mostly done, so he could relax a little. Chris and Paul had never really talked about anything personal. Their meetings had been short and to the point, so they really had nothing in common to talk about.

"Did you see that article in last Sunday's paper?" asked Paul. "Seems like the newspapers are convinced there is a plot to kill some of the Congressmen involved in getting us into Vietnam to start with. I wonder if it's a green beret gone off the rails." Chris nodded. Paul continued, "It's going to be a lot tougher now. The President has ordered secret service protection for those who had been in office as the war started. What an insane project."

"Yeah, well I think I'll be getting up to the hospital," said Chris.

"Go ahead," replied Paul. "I'll pick up the tab. Give you a call in about a month."

"Take it easy," waved Chris as he left. The drive to Methodist Hospital was uneventful, giving Chris time to recall the events of the last two days. After he had left the restaurant where Ellie was dining with her boyfriend, he tried to call her when he got home, hoping to find out what, if anything, had happened. There was no answer. He tried again the following morning and still no answer. Finally, he called the dress shop and talked to Mrs. Thoms, who informed him that Ellen had been in a nasty car accident and was at the Methodist Hospital. Upon calling there, he found she could have no visitors until tonight.

Stopping at the nurse's station on the fourth floor, he asked a nurse about the condition of Ellen Nantucket. The nurse pointed to a doctor just coming out of Ellen's room.

"A slightly fractured fibia—er, that is leg, two broken ribs, one of which punctured a lung narrowly missing the heart, a broken nose, a sliced cheek, and assorted contusions."

"Uh, thanks," said Chris. "How bad was she?"

"We almost lost her," replied the doctor. "She lost a lot of blood from the puncture. She's lucky to be here! By the way, she needs rest so don't stay too long—oh, she's going to be alright. She'll mend fast. Don't look so worried." The doctor placed his hand on Chris' shoulder as Chris turned slowly away, thinking.

He hurried down to her room and looked in cautiously. Ellen was watching the door as she heard the footsteps, knowing somehow, the visitor was for her. "Hi," she managed, with a slow wave. A slight smile.

"Jesus, Ellie, are you alright?" Chris looked like he was going to come apart. "God, Ellie, tell me it isn't so."

Ellen was confused. Why did he have such a wild look to him? She was the one who was hurting. "Oh," she said holding her hand out for him, "Chris, I must look a sight." Her speech was slowed by the drugs and bandages. "Come here." He came close enough for her to take his hand. She did. His shoulders and face had the look of someone who had given up. His eyes were burning, brimming with unshed tears. "My face in bandages," she said, "my leg in traction—but I'm okay—I..."

"I did this to you," he mumbled, almost incoherent. "It's my fault!"

"Chris!" Ellen said, as firmly as she could, "Shut up! Listen!" She squeezed his hand as hard as she could. At the same time, he seemed to come out of his trance. She eased the pressure on his hand. He dropped her hand, pulled up a chair to her bed and sat heavily down.

"Ellie, what happened?" he asked, hoping against hope it wasn't as he feared it was.

"I'm not sure, Chris, but it's coming back to me. I was out to dinner with a friend, a man friend, Chris." She looked at the ceiling, then back at Chris with an apologetic smile. "I guess you know I have been dating. It's no secret. And, I like him, Chris, I like him a lot." Chris shifted forward a little, his head hung down, eyes looking at the floor, not seeing anything. "I like you too, Chris, in a different way. Hey, c'mon, look at me," she said softly. "C'mon." He looked up, and she could see the hurt in his expression, the tears in his eyes. "A girl couldn't have a better friend than you, you know that. I depend on you a lot. I miss my brother terribly, sometimes the ache is so big it seems to swallow my whole body. You help make some of that hurt go away. I can never repay you. You are special to me. But, a girl looks for someone to fall into a special kind of love with. I've found him. Oh, Chris, I hope you'll be happy for me."

Chris looked down and wiped his nose with his coat sleeve. Looking up he said,

"Go on, Ellie. The accident."

"Yeah, well, my friend got sick, asked me to get the car and bring it around front so he could get home. Next thing I remember is a nurse telling me where I was and that everything would be okay."

Paul waited a few minutes, staring into the distance, until the waitress brought the check. He was still shook up about Ellen's accident. He thought about it as he drove to the nearby Standard station to fill up. What was going on? Service was slow at the station, but soon he was on his way to Methodist Hospital. He had been there the last two days, but Ellen had been unconscious, then zapped by the drugs. He recalled the feeling of terror as the policeman paged his license number in the restaurant. Apparently, a drifter had run down to the accident and reported to police that the car had come from the restaurant parking lot. He also reported seeing a man in the lot who could have been under the car. It had been too dark for any description, or to be sure.

Paul recalled how tense things were at the hospital and how relieved he was after the surgeon reported her to be in fair condition now, her outlook was excellent. Earlier that day, he had been sitting around, and they told him to come back at 7:00. She would be awake by then, though still medicated. He parked and headed for her room.

He saw the familiar face just as he turned into the doorway. Ellen looked up into his eyes with a big smile, and looked back down at Chris.

"Chris, this is the man I was telling you about." Chris didn't want to turn around very bad, but rose from his chair, turned and let out an audible gasp. He was extending his hand for a handshake, but froze. Paul froze also. Ellen slowly said, "Have—you—two—met?" She was puzzled by the reactions, but under sedation was not as sharp as normal.

"No, ah, no," Paul said. Too loud. Too fast. Then taking Chris' immobile hand he shook it and said, "Paul Grayson—and you are?"

"Stone," Chris mumbled, "Chris Stone." With that he hurried out the door, slamming his shoulder into the doorway corner, then went fleeing down the hallway, down the stairs and out into the sanctuary of the dark night.

Paul was turned around staring at the doorway. He looked at Ellen, then at the doorway, then back at Ellen. Finally, he found his voice. "Ellen, I'm sorry." He gestured helplessly at the door. Ellen was getting dizzy. She laid her head back, closed her eyes and took a deep, painful breath. Paul moved to her side and gently took her hand. He was back in control, at least from outward appearances. He forced his mind to slow down and concentrate on the here and now.

He leaned over, "Ellen," he said softly, "Ellen."

"Yes, Paul, I'm okay," she said weakly, not opening her black and blue eyes.

"Stay with me a minute."

"I'll stay a lot longer than that." She was sleeping.

24

FEBRUARY - APRIL 1975
AFTERMATH

The sound of breaking glass startled Chris. His arm had involuntarily swept a half full bottle of Jack Daniels off the kitchen table. He was still slumped over, resting his head on his forearm. His eyes were now open, not focusing well, but open. The table held the remains of a two-day drunk: three empty whiskey bottles, four glasses and a bag of open spilled potato chips with a grease spot below.

"Jesus!" Chris slowly lifted his head massaging his temple with his left hand, his eyes blinking rapidly to clear his vision. "Jesus H. Keyrist!" He paused for several seconds taking in the scene around him. The cheap, three-room apartment, the kitchen sink with its usual allocation of dirty dishes, glasses, pots, and silverware. The bare overhead bulb forcing its harsh brightness into his consciousness.

He could feel it coming on. The personal recriminations. *How could I have been so blind? So stupid? So dumb? And, then to see Paul, to know that it was him all along. To come so close to killing the only person I had really cared for.* "Jesus!" He was startled by his own voice.

He got up shakily from the kitchen table and made his way, woozily, to the living room couch. He lay down on his back and put his hand on his forehead. *It wouldn't be as bad if a stranger had shown up at the hospital*, he thought. *I could drop Ellie and nobody would know. But now? Ridicule, fingers pointing—who knows? Forget it! Pa was right.*

177

Ain't no woman worth her salt. But, maybe Ellie couldn't help it. Hell, I ain't worth much either. Can't do anything right. Well, that's not entirely true. We've got a couple politicians that aren't going to make mistakes any more. And, you know what? I got me another guy to settle with. Let's get on with it. I'll give her something no one else will. She'll see who really cares, and then it'll be too late.

Ever since the FBI attached a pattern to the killings of the Congressmen, they had quite severe security measures in place. Those who had played an important part in the Vietnam War were protected almost as well as the President. There had been no further attempts.

Chris was determined, but not foolish. Any execution would have to be carried out with great precision. The episode at the hospital made it easier to plan the next mission. He was now expendable. He reached down to plug the phone back in. He dialed hesitantly at first, then with great force. "Ellie?" The hospital switchboard had put him through. "Ellie, how are you feeling?"

"Chris, oh Chris, where have you been? I've tried calling several times—and your father was no help!" she said forcefully.

"Hey, kid, don't worry. I'm fine. I just needed a little time to myself." They talked awhile about Ellen's condition. "Ellie, did Steve ever talk politics with you? You know, mention anyone he blamed for the war?" Chris didn't like to bring Steve up at this time, but Ellie had talked with him about Steve several times. He knew Ellie had lost a big part of her when Steve was killed; killed by the same people that had killed his friends and many more. It was the bond that tied Chris to Ellie these past two years. A common loss. He would sacrifice himself to help make her whole again. After all, he thought, I damn near killed her. The tears were close for him, again. *Damn near killed a sweet,*

178

defenseless little sister. How stupid! The rage of his mistake was building within him again. He clenched his fist, swallowed hard and continued. "I'm doing some, ah, research and I just wondered."

"You know Chris, he never said much about it. He just wanted to serve his country the best way he could." She found her tongue growing thick, "But, he did mention a Senator Cambridge as being more communist than American. He really didn't care for him."

After hanging up, Chris started cleaning up the apartment. *Senator Cambridge from Michigan, yes.* Chris knew a lot about him. Cambridge had already been checked out. *He's from a small town in central Michigan. Usually is back in Michigan the first part of each month. Because of his Vietnam posture, he is reported to be under heavy guard.*

"Get your right wing up. That's it. Make lots of small corrections, not one big one." Chris was enjoying his first flight lesson, soaring through the cloudy sky on an early March afternoon. He had always wanted to fly anyway, so this was fun. The flight instructor was a mild-mannered, easy going, middle-aged man. Chris hadn't picked him, specifically. He was more interested in location. He needed a small, rural airport that had flight instruction and planes to rent. It had to be within a hundred miles of Centralia, Michigan – home of Senator Cambridge.

It was no problem for Chris to take two weeks from work under the guise of attending a seminar and equipment auction, as he had done several times before. Then, he would drive over for a couple long weekends to finish up. In a month's time, he would know all he needed to know about flying the Piper Cherokee.

His instructor talked him through several maneuvers. Chris caught on quickly. Chris was a good student, breezing through his next nine lessons with help from his good-natured instructor. After several touch and goes on a sunny, still, cold day, the instructor said, "Pull up by the office and let me out. You take her around the patch." Chris gulped. He was confident alright, but still....*alone?*

"All alone?" he said much more casually than he felt.

"Yep. Nothin' to it. You done it yourself the last ten times anyway." Chris let him off then taxied to the end of the runway. There was no tower and no traffic either, but Chris took a careful look around anyway, before lining up on the centerline. The radio work done, he moved the throttle forward all the way and felt the excitement growing within as the Cherokee picked up speed. He watched the speed increase – 40...50...70. Gently pulling back on the yoke, he broke contact with the ground. *Let's see, climb to 2100, turn, continue climbing to 2800.*

He found himself pretending the instructor was next to him giving instructions. A small downdraft felt like a 200 foot drop, though he knew it was probably only 20. *Around the patch, upwind, crosswind, downwind, and then the final leg. Steady now.* Wiping his palms, he checked his speed as he tried to find the proper glide path to bring him over the threshold. *A little more power, too much, another boost, there, it looks good. Drop the nose—not too much. Contact! When did I start sweating*, he thought. Whew. The radio came to life startling him.

"Comanche N4547 cleared for another go-around." It was his instructor. *Okay, if that's what he wants.* Chris pushed the throttle forward once again. After the fourth go-around, he pulled up to the gas pump, climbed down, and found his knees shakier than he thought.

He steadied himself with the wing just as his instructor came around.

Handshakes and accolades completed, they headed for the office. Before he knew it, the ground crew had pulled his shirt out and cut off the shirt tail right below the last button. An old tradition, it was explained, after completing your first solo. Then, to be tacked to the office bulletin board.

"Now, when can I practice?" asked Chris.

"Most anytime old '47 is around. Should be a day without too much wind 'cause we got to work some more dual on crosswind landings. Otherwise, give me a call first. Okay?"

"Yah, sounds good." Chris exchanged pleasantries a few minutes, then took off for his motel room.

Senator Cambridge didn't mind the attention at all. He could use all the exposure he could get. He had a tough race coming up next year. His Vietnam stance had backfired on him. He thought that by siding with the North and ridiculing the military he would be solidifying his position. He found out the loudmouths he listened to were very vocal— and very few. The majority of his constituents held quite a different view than his. The executions of his fellow lawmakers would certainly garner him some sympathy votes, plus his acting the part of the reluctant interviewee actually got him more exposure. The media flocked after someone who appeared not to want to talk to them.

So, with two State Trooper cars behind and one Secret Service SUV ahead, he felt secure. This scene was repeated each time he flew from DC to Grand Rapids, then drove to Centralia and on through six more miles to the family farm. *What had it been*, he thought, *six times with all this fuss?* He smiled.

The troopers and agents were keeping a close watch on all the side roads, groves and ditches. The route had been cleared an hour earlier but none of them wanted an incident on their record. You could hardly blame them if they missed a little black spot up in the sky to the west of them, framed by the sun, coming up from behind.

You got to have a little luck, thought Chris, as he scanned the instrument panel.

A clear, crisp early spring afternoon. *The Senator's right on schedule. The plane was available, the sun's at my back.* The miniature motorcade had just left Centralia city limits and was crawling along like so many child's toys, the white top of the Senator's red and white Cadillac convertible clearly visible.

Chris wrestled with his decision all night long. *But dammit, this is war, too. How many people just like me died in Nam? Like Steve? Like Harry, and Al, and so many others? Don't I owe them something? Should the few old men who sent us to die escape? You're damn right they should pay. Well, I'm getting my share.*

Exactly one month after his first flight lesson, he proficiently lined up the Cherokee on the highway centerline just like the runway. He adjusted the throttle and started his downward dive, using the car behind the Cadillac as the moving threshold. The cars were becoming bigger and bigger. He noticed some heads poking out the side windows of the Secret Service SUV. The troopers had turned on their rotating lights. The Senator's car swerved at the last second, but it just made the impact that much more effective. The Cherokee's propeller rotated fiercely through the thin fabric of the convertible roof, slicing through the rear seat, separating an arm from a shoulder and a knee from a leg, ripping a wide gash in the chest of the Senator before coming to rest halfway through the 500 cubic inch Cadillac engine.

The angle of the car and force of the crash caused the car to roll into the fairly steep ditch on the right side of the road. The car rolled on top of the plane's fuselage, separating it from the wings, causing gallons of aviation fuel to pour on the lighted ash of the Senator's cigar.

25

APRIL 1975
GONE

The morning was extremely warm for early April. The wind was quiet and the sun bright at 8:00 in the morning. He planned to get to work at 10:00 today. Paul took the morning paper and a cup of coffee out to the terrace. Settling down, he glanced at the headlines: "Senator Killed in Fiery Car-Plane Crash." In smaller headlines: "Minnesota man piloting plane also killed. Police and FBI believe the dead pilot to be the 'Congressional Killer,' responsible for at least five executions." Paul set the want ads on the seat of the wrought iron chair, then settled into the full article, crossing his legs, sipping the hot coffee and reading on. "My God!" he exclaimed out loud. "Can't be!" *He doesn't know how to fly*, thought Paul, *but that's his middle name.* He continued reading about how the pilot was thrown clear and identified by fingerprints, as he carried no identification and the plane was completely burned.

He left his coffee, went back into the house, grabbed the phone and dialed. "Stone Construction," growled a voice on the other end.

"Yes—er, is Chris Stone available?" A silence on the other end, "Hello? You there?"

"Yah," the voice said a lot quieter. "We, ah, we understand Chris, ah, died in a plane crash yesterday afternoon. Who is this?"

Paul let the phone trail down the side of his face as his eyes took on a vacant stare. "Hey, who is this? You there?" Paul looked at the phone like it was poison, slammed it onto the receiver and ran out to the terrace. Grabbing the paper he looked for the sentence that burned in his mind. There it is! "Senator Cambridge, well known for his anti-military posture during the Vietnam War..."

Paul tore through the kitchen, past his startled mother and hollered back, "Look, Mom, tell Dad I won't be in today—okay? Something has just come up. I'll tell you about it later." He ran to his room, grabbed his address book, and raced for Chris' apartment.

Paul had never been to Chris' apartment, but had no trouble finding it. It was the north upstairs apartment in a low-rent fourplex. He drove by slowly, observing but pretending not to pay any attention to it. He turned the corner, the apartment now hidden by another similar building, and parked. He walked through the backyards, in the back door and up the back steps. All was quiet.

He knew that if he suspected a link in the killings, so would others, and if they hadn't already been to this apartment they soon would be. He tried the door knob, then a gentle knock. Finally he slipped a credit card out and managed to slip the latch back.

Opening the door slightly, he eased inside and quietly closed the door. "Hello," he said quietly at first, then repeated it loudly. Confident nobody was in the apartment, he gingerly walked into the kitchen, taking in the smell and looking at the waste basket full of bottles. Paul fervently wished he had tried harder to get a hold of Chris after the hospital episode.

He went to the sliding glass door, looked out, unlocked it, and noticed steps down from the deck. Now he had an escape route if needed.

Paul went to the imitation rolltop desk he saw in the living room, jimmied the latch and lifted it up. Searching through the normal contractor's plans and papers, he discovered a plain manila envelope with no writing on it. Opening it, he saw many newspaper articles – all of them about Congressmen who had been killed by an unknown "Congressional Executioner." Inside was a file folder with the names of ten Congressmen, and four names "X'd" out. Paul sat down on the office chair, head bowed down, one arm on the desk, the file folder hanging over the arm of the chair, brushing the floor.

"My God in heaven," cried Paul in a coarse whisper, "what kind of monster did I create?" He started to sob. At first separated by several seconds of thought and quiet, but then the sobs were continuous, racking his body from top to bottom.

Deep, gut-wrenching sobs. Finally he slipped to the floor, sprawled out, face down.

The sobs became more irregular as the futility of his actions surfaced.

Just then he heard keys jangling. A voice, fairly loud, said, "I don't know if I should let you guys in or not!"

"Look we showed you our papers—you know who to call."

"Yah, yah..."

Paul headed for the sliding door, closed it quietly, leaped over the side of the deck to the ground about 8 feet down and strode briskly out of the line of sight. On the way home he debated whether to tell Ellen of Chris' death. As of yet he didn't think she was aware that he and Chris knew each other, so he would have no reason to pay any attention to a Christopher Stone, pilot from Minnesota.

What a mess. Ellen just about kills herself with my car, Chris has been on some private crusade of his own killing Congressmen right and left, and I've been feeding him. Unknowingly giving support to the idea that we could take the law into our own hands. Sure, I wasn't advocating killing anybody. But, then it's just a matter of degree, isn't it? I was willing to rob not only money, but my father of his good name. Am I any less guilty, or more? I instigated the first meeting. I came up with the plan that kept us going. Christ, what a mess. I must be like the plague.

Ellen was reading Paul's note for the third time.

My Dearest Ellen,

Do not blame yourself in any way for what I am about to do and say. It's beyond your control and now it's beyond mine. It's the hardest thing I have ever had to do in my life.

I must tell you how much I love you. I am not saying this to make our parting harder but to let you know it IS because I love you so much I must be strong and carry through.

I have been a part of some situations that have had terrible complications. These things I can tell no one about. I alone, must carry the burden to my grave. I would not ask, expect, or allow any other person to share in this burden. The consequences of my actions are far reaching and horrible to contemplate.

Please do not try to reach me. I will soon be gone for several months, and when (and if) I return, I will be unresponsive to your communications for your own good.

Enough about me. More about you. Ellen, you are a precious human being. You brought happiness and stability to my life. What you have been and what you have meant to me I cannot express in words.

You must, I repeat, must—share your outlook, attitude and spirit with the world. Shake off any hurts I may have caused you, cope a little better with the loss of Steve, and continue to be a rainbow in this world of rainy days.

All my love, respect, admiration and best wishes. Have a great life!
Paul

This is all so confusing, she thought, as she sat in her kitchen with her mending leg in a brace and elevated a bit, numbed by the letter. She looked at the envelope. It had no stamp, so Paul must have dropped it off himself. She tried to reach him at his office and home. Both places advised her the same thing. Paul Grayson would not be available for an unknown time.

She was at a loss. What was *so* terrible that Paul could not talk to her about it? *Does he have a terminal disease? Is he going to marry somebody else? What is it? We've shared so many things these past two years. I've certainly given him no reason not to trust me, to confide in me. The last several months have been great. We even talked of marriage. What happened?*

She reached for the phone and dialed Chris' number. She didn't like to burden Chris. He was seemingly off in his own world these last six months, but she wanted to talk to somebody. He was a good listener. He had been gone for a couple weeks to some auction, or something, his dad had told her. No answer.

Calling Stone Construction brought immediate results. A woman answered. "Is Chris there? Or Matt?" asked Ellen.

"Who's calling?" a smoker's voice asked.

"This is Ellen Nantucket, a friend of Chris'," she added.

"Well, honey, I've got bad news for you. Chris was killed yesterday in an airplane accident in Michigan."

"Oh my God!" croaked Ellen, "Oh, my God!"

"Funeral is Monday, 2:00 at the St. Paul Central United Methodist Church."

"What, what's that again?" The information was repeated for Ellen until she got it down.

I can't believe this, thought Ellen, as she absent-mindedly put on a sweater and headed for her car. She was out to her car when she realized she had no place to go. She found herself wiping away a few tears with her sleeve as she made her way back to her apartment. She flung herself on her couch as the torrent of tears came. She had no desire to stop them.

26

Jim was sitting on his couch, beer in hand, wondering if he should lay a big burden on Sara. This would be a turning point in their relationship, he knew. *Well, not tonight, but Friday after we get back from our big two-person birthday party.* He was going to invite her up to his apartment and ask her to accompany him to Minneapolis.

After returning from Baltimore in February, he had been very depressed. Actually this made him work physically harder, but there wasn't much progress. He remembered the day like yesterday, even though it was seven or eight months ago. Sara came in as usual, but was very quiet. She told Jim they had a consult about him and that X-rays showed a problem in the spine that probably was holding progress back. An operation could improve his chances to walk again, or could result in paralysis: 75% chance for a good result, 25% chance for a bad result.

It had taken him ten seconds to opt for the operation, because the way he was going was no way to live. Sara agreed and said she would be with him every step of the way, which was a great comfort.

On Wednesday, October 2, the operation was performed. It ended up being as successful as the doctors had hoped. Rehab went quite well after that with measurable progress almost every day. By January, he was walking with just the aid of two special arm canes. But better than that, his memory was coming back.

In early January, he had news for Sara. "Sara, I think I know who I

190

am."

"Jim, we know who you are, you just have to get stronger, and you can get your own place and be independent. You're almost there."

"No, it's much more than that. What I am about to tell you has to be between us, but I need you to find a way to verify it, okay?"

"Yes, sure," said Sara, with a puzzled expression.

"I'm pretty sure I am not Sergeant James E. Tonger, USAF, but Steve Nantucket, Captain, USAF. I'm not from Baltimore, but from Minneapolis. After my back operation, things started to come to me. I've had suspicions for a while, but didn't dare say anything. I don't know why I was identified as Sergeant Tonger, if I'm not. But, if I try to go through channels with this, they'll probably put me in a psych ward. But, you could investigate on your own until we have some kind of proof."

"My God, Jim—er, Steve. Are you pretty sure? It's not a dream?"

"No, I can recall some events from living in Minneapolis. My parents were killed in a car crash when I was like 17 years old. I had a younger sister I took care of. I joined the Air Force when she went to college. I'm sure. But I need some kind of proof. And, how did I end up being Sergeant Tonger?"

Sara sat still and stared at the wall for twenty seconds. "I'll do it. You know I would do anything to help you Jim, gosh—I mean Steve. Well, for now you still better be Jim, okay?"

"Good idea."

Sara came to work the next day with an idea. One of her previous patients had returned to the Air Force and was an Air Force lawyer. He had told Sara if there was anything he could ever do, to call him. It was time to take him up on that offer. She had to leave a message, but he called back in the afternoon. She explained the situation, gave him the two names involved, and asked him to get on it as fast as he could. He promised he would. "Anything for you," he told her.

The wait was stressful on both Jim and Sara, but in the first part of February, she got a visit from a Major Stephenson. He arranged to meet with both Sara and Jim.

"Jim, by the way your name is Steve, Steve Nantucket. So, I'll call you Steve from now on if that's okay. We found two people who were involved with the shoot-down and your attempted rescue. You bailed out and landed in enemy territory. Fortunately, we had a squad not that far away. They got to your site, then had to dig in, as the VC also spotted the activity. They lobbed some mortars, and Sergeant Tonger and others were killed. You were injured and knocked out. Two of the survivors knew how badly pilots and officers were treated by the VC. They could see that you and Sergeant Tonger were fairly similar, so they took Sergeant Tonger's dog tags and uniform and traded his for yours. You three were the only survivors and were soon captured. They split you up into different prison camps, so you never knew what happened to each other."

"Thanks, Major. I knew something was off with this whole thing, but I didn't know what. Now I do. What a load off."

They visited more about paperwork and procedure, then the Major left.

"My God, uh, Steve, what are you going to do now?"

"Good question. How soon am I going to get out of here?"

"You didn't hear it from me, but I heard in about two weeks."

Sara's prediction came true, as he was notified about his release and that the VA had some apartments that newly-released patients could stay in for up to three months, if needed. It was all furnished, and after getting some groceries, it was good enough for him. The walking was getting better. He did not have to use his canes except if he got really tired. It would never be one hundred percent, but it was far better than he expected a year ago.

A couple days later, Sara Forsyth was giggling like a teenager. She was enjoying her wine and her company. "Steve, cut it out! If you tell me one more Ole and Lena joke, I'll split!" Steve offered to take Sara out to dinner on her birthday. She finally accepted. He liked her a lot, but not just because she was my nurse, he convinced himself, but because Sara was Sara. He was glad to be with her. Soon their dinner was served. After dinner, wine was ordered and the appropriate toasts were made.

Sara even got Steve out on the dance floor. He couldn't dance, of course, but he could shuffle his feet to the music and vigorously move his upper body and arms to the music. You could tell he couldn't walk normally, as he had a halting gait. Sara was the only one in the place who knew his limp was a miracle. No one she knew ever worked harder and with more purpose to rehabilitate himself than Steve.

Afterward, Steve invited Sara up to his apartment for birthday cake. He had not really been able to put a move on Sara. He couldn't read her signals. He was sure that she liked him, but how much? "Sara, ever since I found out what happened in Nam, and who I am, I've been fighting with this problem. I need your help…again."

He sat down beside her on the couch offering her a glass of wine with one hand and putting the other behind her, on the couch back. He looked at her. Flush cheeks, perfect complexion, tipped up nose, but more than that as evidenced by her chosen profession, a caring person. *All I have dreamed of,* he thought. *Ellie would like her a lot.* They were much alike.

"I told you about my parents being killed and how Ellie and I became so close. I know I have to go to Minnesota and find her. I've thought it over. I just can't wait any longer. I couldn't just call her, I can't write. It's just too much. I have to go in person. Whatever I do, can you imagine what it will be like for her when she sees me after thinking I've been dead for these years? I have to be there. I'd like you to come with me. It's asking a lot, I know, but I could use your support. Would you consider it?"

Sara set her wine glass down on the walnut coffee table as she slowly got up and walked toward the window with her hands clasped behind her back. From the third story she could see the lights of Foresters' Park a block away. Most apartments were dark, but here and there she could see a light on. She half turned her body, her fingers playing with her gold chain necklace, a present from Dr. McKenny.

Looking at Jim, or Steve, she saw a vulnerable Midwestern boy. *Oh, he was a man*, she thought. *Make no mistake about that.* But, she knew much more than that. She saw a happy, blond, blue-eyed 6'-2" athletic-looking man. Inside that body was more determination than she knew existed. How had he defied doctors' predictions? How had he gone through his prescribed strenuous rehabilitation routines, and, where others begged to stop, he asked for more? And now, he was walking. Not perfect, but walking. *I think*, she continued, *it was so he could get back to his Ellie – to make sure she would be all right.*

He was sitting on the edge of the couch, waiting. She turned back to the window, but this time she saw nothing. Her eyes were focused a thousand miles away.

"Steve," she started, still looking away, "I may have been terribly cruel to you."

"No way," Steve said loudly. "You have done more for me already than any person has a right to expect."

She turned and held up her hand like a stop sign. "Let me continue. I like you a lot Jim, I mean Steve," she laughed nervously. "It gave me great professional pleasure to see your progress; to see you defy the predictions and walk again. In the process, I got personally involved. And, you are one of the most fabulous people I know, so it was easy, too easy. But, it can't go on." She walked over to an easy chair across from Steve, plopped down, looked at the floor and continued. "I've had to make some painful decisions lately, too."

She recalled her conversation with Rod the previous night. He had been supportive of Sara and her relationship with Steve at first, "But now that Steve is back among the living mentally and physically," he had reminded her, "you can start seeing less of him and more of me." He was right, too. She had gone overboard, unintentionally leading Steve on. It just happened. But, the results were the same. *I love Dr. Rodney McKenny*, she thought. *This is the right life for me.*

"Dr. McKenny and I, well, we plan on getting married in the near future. I love him – I really do!" She noticed his immediate look of surprise and a red blush creeping up his neck and face. "I like you too, Steve. I hope we can be good friends. I...I—so you see, I can't go with you."

She got up to walk over to Steve just as he got up and headed for the kitchen, avoiding her eyes. She watched him go. In a minute he came back with the wine bottle, brushed past her, filled her glass, then his. He headed for the window. "Look Sara, you can still go with me if you choose. I have to do this. I need your help. I don't even have a car." He looked back at her, standing near the coffee table.

"Don't make it hard on us, Steve. I can't go. It would ruin my career at the hospital, my future with Dr. McKenny...there are too many things I've worked on for too long to throw it all away now."

He looked out the window. "Our relationship is complicated, Sara, I think I fell for you, but maybe it's just because I am so grateful for your support as I got better. I was thinking of something more for the two of us, but I didn't know about Dr. McKenny. No matter what, I have to get to Minnesota before I can move on. If you came with me, we could sort a lot out." Nothing was said for a good minute.

"I am so sorry it came to this Steve, but here," she continued' "if you want to drive, take my car." Her outstretched hand offered him the keys. He made no move to accept them, just kept staring out the window. "Steve," she jangled the keys. He kept staring out the window. She placed them on the corner of the coffee table. "Well, it's been nice. I'll be going," she said softly as she stooped down to pick up her purse. She headed for the door, hesitated, and walked over to him and gave him a light kiss on the cheek. He did not move, but she tasted his salty tear on her lips. "I'll take a taxi home. The keys are on the coffee table. Please take my car. It's the least I can do," she said as she started to cry. She opened the door and slipped into the hall, pausing a second to look back at the rigid figure of a man at the window.

The door closing jarred Steve into action. He grabbed a suitcase from the closet, took his money from the hiding place, and grabbed the bag which was still mostly packed from the hospital. With Sara's car keys in hand, he headed down the hallway with an ungainly, but purposeful, walk.

Five hours later, on the outskirts of Pittsburgh, he located a motel, and with the sun just coming up, he fell asleep. After waking at 2:00 in the afternoon, he decided to drive only as far as Toledo. He realized he still didn't have much stamina. After leaving Toledo, he headed for Madison. The roads were icy in the morning, but by noon they had cleared up. The forecast was for more unseasonably cold April weather today, followed by unseasonably warm weather tomorrow.

Heading for Minneapolis on the seventh of April, Steve forced himself to think things through for the hundredth time. *First, Ellie's name with an address should be in the phone book. Then, I'll get near her place and call from a gas station to see if she's home. I won't tell her who I am. I don't know a better way to handle this. I don't want to scare her, or worse, but knowing her, she can handle it. Maybe she doesn't even live in Minneapolis anymore...or maybe she's married and her name is different. What then? I can always call that dress shop she worked at. The old gal there will know where Ellie is.*

He continued driving towards the Twin Cities, with stomach churning and palms sweating. He would wipe them off, and one minute later they were sweaty again. *I don't think so*, he said to himself. *I don't think she got married. Just a feeling. Speaking of marriage...* He had given it some thought for he and Sara. He felt the right chemistry when they were together. But, Sara must not have. *I'm afraid I behaved badly the night of her birthday*, he thought. But, it was such a shock. *Dr. McKenny? Hard to believe. Oh, he was an all right guy, but not Sara's style, in my humble opinion. Unless he's a lot different than I think.*

The skyline of Minneapolis-St. Paul loomed larger in his windshield and a fresh nervousness pervaded Steve's whole body. He found a phone book at a small gas station, found her Bloomington address and phone number, gave a sigh and wrote the information down.

She must have an apartment in the same area where we grew up, thought Steve. *The address is somewhat familiar.* He headed around the beltline towards a Standard station he knew, which should only be a couple blocks from her apartment. Glancing at his watch, it registered 12:30. Half an hour to the station, then the phone call to see if Ellie was home.

Ellen looked at her reflection in the mirror. *Basic black. Funeral black. Plain and simple.* She didn't want to go to Chris' funeral, but she knew she must. He deserves at least this from me. She had not been to work since she received Paul's note. She checked in by phone with Mrs. Thoms this morning and explained about the funeral and that she would be back at work on Monday morning.

Putting on her coat, she noticed the time was 1:00 as the apartment door closed behind her. *Is that my phone?* She thought she heard it ringing, but knew she better get going. *It's a good half hour to 45 minutes to the church in St. Paul.* She hesitated, started back, and then thinking better of it, headed for her car.

Steve let the phone ring twelve times before hanging up. Searching for another coin, he thought, *she's not at work*, he had tried there first, *but I can call and ask for the boss lady.* He called only to find out that Mrs. Thoms would not be back until 2:00. Could she take a message? "No thanks, I'll call back," he told her.

He killed the hour by gassing up the car and driving to a coffee shop. He was too nervous to eat, but nursed a cup of coffee. Finally 2:00 came and he called the shop. Yes, Mrs. Thoms knew where Ellen was.

"Who wants to know?" she had asked.

"An old college friend from the U of M, just passing through," he lied.

"Well, okay. She is at a funeral at the St. Paul Central United Methodist Church."

Steve wanted to ask her all kinds of questions, but thinking better of it, simply thanked her and hung up.

Paul waited until the last minute before he slipped into the back pew. He did not want to face Ellen, but felt an overwhelming obligation to attend both the church service and the graveside service. He knew he could escape Ellen here at the church service. If she chose to go to the graveside service, he would not be able to avoid her, but he could ignore her. What a dark day this is, he thought, and it could get a lot worse. He could come late to the grave site, and leave early. As the church service concluded, Paul slipped out the doors and around the corner to his car.

Ellen stood up, wiped the tears from her eyes, and turned around. She saw the back of a familiar figure just as it disappeared from view. But, the ushers were dismissing the mourners row by row, so she could only wait her turn. As soon as she got outside, she looked around to see if it had really been Paul. It looked like him, but she could easily have been mistaken. She headed for her car to be ready to follow in the funeral procession.

Driving along, she rolled her window down to take in the warm breeze. The sun was shining brightly, warming the earth. She briefly wondered about the feeling a person would have if they were down in the coffin, alive, hearing the dirt hit the coffin lid. *My God, what a stupid thought.*

Paul waited until the procession was five minutes ahead of him. He knew the way to the cemetery and wanted to come in last so he could leave first. He checked the rearview mirror since he was going to pull out from between two cars. A car was coming, so he waited for it to pass. Instead, it stopped short and waved him out. Must want my spot, he thought. As he pulled out, he waved a thanks to the driver and sped towards the cemetery.

Mighty friendly drivers around here, mused Steve, as he parallel-parked in the recently vacated spot. The church looked mostly empty, but Steve was sure somebody would be around with the information he wanted. He was given directions to the cemetery by a kind old lady who was still wondering, "Why anybody would ever get into one of them little airplanes anyway." *Whatever that meant*, thought Steve.

Paul backed his car just inside the cemetery gate and walked over towards the small crowd, just as the service started. He stood toward the back and didn't look up until after the prayer. When he looked up, he was looking right into Ellen's eyes across the casket. Their eyes locked for a moment before Paul looked away and stepped a half step to his left, shielding his face from Ellen. As he glanced to make sure she could not see him, he noticed a fairly tall, slender woman just behind and to the left of Ellen. She had on large dark sunglasses, a black stocking cap and dark coat. He had never seen her before and got the sense she was not family.

Steve drove slowly towards the cemetery entrance. An electric anticipation coursed through his body. His nerves were tingling. He could tell she was here. He wanted to see her first, to ease into the situation. God, he couldn't wait. *Together again. Someone to trust, to lean on, to share with.* He pulled around a car faced out. Ready for a quick get-a-way, chuckled Steve, breaking a little tension. He pulled in right beside it, got out and leaned against the driver's door. He could see the group about 100 yards away, but could not make out Ellie.

He would wait.

Then, from upwind they heard it: a lone bugler started playing taps. The pastor stopped right before the last prayer. Ellen had heard of such a situation. There he stood, upwind, about 100 yards away, dressed entirely in black, his head surrounded by a black cowl and eyes shielded with black sunglasses. Rumor had it he appeared at funerals for veterans who were not having an official military funeral, played taps, and then disappeared. Everyone was mesmerized by the hauntingly beautiful rendition.

Ellen had memorized some words from a poem by K. Robert Kloos, synchronizing them with taps, and she sang along in her mind as the bugle played in the background.

I'm Here

Full of Grace

Gave My Best

Like All the Rest

But Here I Am

My Final Rest

God Bless America I Died for You

As the last note trailed off, Steve made his way closer to the small crowd. The pastor started on the last prayer. Then a tall, well-dressed man started to slowly break away from the group as the prayer was ending. A lady circled around the group and intercepted him. It was Ellie! Yes! *By all the heaven's Saints, it's her!*

201

"Paul Grayson, you stop right now and listen. You listen good!" He stopped, but would not look at her. "You left me without giving me a chance. There is no trouble so big that I don't deserve a chance to help you. You are important to me, Paul. I love you. I haven't been able to love anybody since Steve. He was taken from me through no choice of his. *You* have a choice."

Paul started walking slowly towards his car, not responding. Ellen followed along talking intently to Paul, not paying any attention to the man with the strange walk, coming slowly towards her, tears streaming down his face.

Paul glanced at the man, eyes drawn toward him because of his halting walk and tear-stained face. Paul thought the man might be coming to talk to him. He dismissed that thought, as he did not recognize him at all. Ellen grabbed Paul's arm and stopped. "Paul, she said quietly, firmly, "if you don't let me help you, nobody else will." She let go as he started, again, for his car. She buried her face in her hands, sobbing.

Strong, familiar arms surrounded her pulling her towards a waiting shoulder.

"Missy, Missy," the voice said, "come here."

27

APRIL, 1975
HOME, AT LAST

Ellen's head was swirling, the earth was spinning and she felt weak. Then nothing. But, the arms held her safely. Paul saw that Ellen had collapsed, so he turned back to where the stranger was holding her. "You know her?" Paul said, warily.

"Yes, I'm ah...let's say, an old friend of the family. She's fainted. I hope that's all it is. Would be obliged if you could help. My legs aren't too good."

"Sure. If you're sure it's nothing serious, we could head for her apartment. I'm Paul Grayson, by the way." Paul offered his hand and Steve gave it a hearty shake. "And you are?"

"For now, I'm Jim Tonger. It's a long story. I'll fill you in back at Ellie's place." On the way to Ellen's they rode in suspicious silence. Paul was thinking of the strange turn of events and coming to the realization that all he really wanted in life was right in front of him. How could he be so blind! He had to find a way to make it work. *Maybe Ellen is through with me. Have I ruined that too?*

Ellen was still out as they placed her carefully on the bed. Steve and Paul went to the kitchen where Steve told his story. Paul sat there, dumbfounded. "Unbelievable," he muttered, almost in shock. "Oh, you told me enough so I believe you, but how can we handle this from Ellen's point of view?" They heard a low moan from the bedroom. "You stay here, would you Steve? I'm going to see what condition she is in before we attempt this." He went into her bedroom just as she was sitting up.

"Paul! What are you doing here? How did I...?" She was rubbing her temples, but got up shakily, and threw her arms around him. "I'm so glad you're here!"

He held her tightly and stroked her hair as he gave a short version of what happened, leaving out Steve's involvement for now. "I've decided to be around here quite a bit, if you'll have me," he replied.

"I'm so mixed up Paul, I dreamt that Steve was holding me in his arms. It was so real. I would swear it really happened! Am I going crazy?" She looked at him with a pleading look.

"Sit down Ellen, I want to tell you an incredible story." He told as much of the story as he could, as if it happened to somebody else, but didn't get too far.

She spoke slowly as with each word a realization was dawning. "You, mean—Steve…could be alive? You really think so?"

"Yes, Ellen, look at me." He took both her hands in his. "Steve is the man I just told you about, who traded dog tags after that terrible war accident, just about died, got amnesia, went through rehab, finally recovered his memory…and came home."

"It *was* him," she said quietly. "It was *him*! OHMYGOD! OHMYGOD! OH MY GOD!" she screamed. "Oh——my——God! It *is* him," she said more quietly, as she fought for control, swallowing and blinking rapidly. Very quietly she said to Paul, "Is he here?" Paul nodded, just as Steve came into the room and swept her into his arms.

"Missy, I missed you so much!"

About the time the 727 was over Chicago en route to Minneapolis from Washington DC, Dr. McKenny was reading a letter of resignation from nurse Sara Forsyth. The only part he didn't understand was the remark about needing the rest of her life to find her car—and the man who took it.

The next day was like a half dream to Ellen. Paul stayed over, and he and Steve were visiting at the kitchen table early in the morning. The memory-provoking smell of bacon and eggs soon brought Ellen into the hall. Noticing her standing in a dreamlike trance, Steve moved to her. His radiant smile was soon returned and a warm, urgent hug was in process. Paul busied himself with the bacon and eggs.

"Steve, oh Steve. I'm still not sure this is real." She pushed him away at arm's length and appraised him from head to foot and back again, shaking her head from side to side. "You look so good!"

"Well, it's true Missy, and I'm staying for a few days, so you'll just have to put up with me."

"Paul, hey. Good morning." She went to get a hug from him and said, "Give me five minutes and I'll take over." Five minutes later, with combed hair and new lipstick, she was true to her word. She gave him a peck on the cheek and took the spatula from Paul. "Am I glad to see you two guys! My two most favorite guys in the whole world. Right here in my own apartment."

Soon breakfast was over, the dishes stacked and only the second cup of coffee remained to be shared. Ellen convinced Steve to stay in her apartment for at least a couple weeks until he could make some plans. Paul was going to work on Tuesday, but would stop over in the evenings. There was going to be plenty to do. Ball games, shopping, driving around, cookouts, and hanging out. They would help each other heal from the hurts of the past.

The next several days were fantastic. Everybody got along, it was a warm Minnesota April, not too windy and lots of sun. Steve and Ellen adjusted to each other like they had never been apart. Cleaning together, shopping together, walking together, even laughing at the same unspoken humor as they had done before. One evening, Paul came over with his guitar. It was an evening to remember, full of wine, joy and songs. Paul was still dreading "the talk" he and Ellen would have, but there would be plenty of time for that.

Ellen visited the store Monday, and Mrs. Thoms was so overjoyed to hear of Steve's story, she had no problem agreeing to give her more time off.

Steve announced he was supposed to go to the VA Hospital the next day for an overnight stay. Because he had POW injuries, they wanted to check him over good and get a baseline for any future problems.

Paul leaned into Ellen and whispered, "Looks like we have the apartment to ourselves tomorrow night, you want to make out?" he chuckled.

"Bad timing, Paul, I'm afraid. There is somebody I really want you to meet, and she'll just be in town tomorrow night. You'll come, won't you? Please," she whispered.

"If you feel that strongly about it, I'll be there. Where are we meeting?"

"Just come over here about 5:00 and we'll go together. But, don't tell anybody. Not everyone in this family appreciates her."

Paul showed up right on time, dressed in tan slacks and an attractive light sweater. As they got into Paul's car, Ellen remarked, "You look so handsome! I am the luckiest girl in the world!"

If you're showering me with compliments already, this girl must be a loser."

"No, no—well, judge for yourself, but I think you will like her. At least I hope so. Go to the Embassy Suites, right off the interstate. You know the one. She is not going to be back until 5:30 or 6:00. But, I have a key and she bought some wine. We can help ourselves.

It didn't take long and they were parked and on the way up to the twelfth floor. It was still light out, but inside the blackout curtains had been pulled and two candles were flickering, casting a romantic mood in the suite. Ellen went to the fridge and pulled out a bottle of wine and poured two glasses. She raised her glass to Paul's, clinked and said, "Here's to us."

"Just relax, I'm going to visit the ladies room."

"I can do that. Who is this girl, anyway?"

"She'll be here pretty soon, then it will be clear. Hang on, I'll be right back—oh, start the music, will you? My friend said we would enjoy what she picked." As Ellen shut the bedroom door she could hear the Hawaiian strings start up.

Paul sat back in an easy chair just relaxing. After several minutes, he started thinking—*glass of wine, candles flickering, Hawaiian music playing, something is going on here*. Just then, Ellen opened the bedroom door and from the dark into the candlelight, she appeared like an angel. She was dressed in her gold-flecked Hawaiian dress. She grabbed Paul's hand, directed him to the hard kitchen floor and said, "Would you dance with me?"

"S-sure" he stuttered, looking around like Ellen's friend might come in at any time. He took her in his arms and they started a slow dance.

"How do you like the new girl?"

"Well, what about...?"

"Relax, sweetheart, it's just you and me and we've got the whole night."

"Oh my God, you got me. Got me good," he said as he settled in closer.

"Yes, I hope you like the surprise. Because I miss you so much, and love you so much, and I love being able to say it without any guilt." She pulled him tight as they stopped dancing and started kissing. She didn't want to stop. He didn't want to stop. Finally they came up for air.

They were enjoying dancing to the Hawaiian music, clinging to each other, kissing, rubbing...

"I don't want to spoil the mood," Paul said, after a while, "but under your dress—something's different."

"Yes it is. You know what?" she caressed his cheek, "If you want to find out you know what you'll have to do."

"You look so beautiful in that dress, especially with the candlelight flickering, I hate to disturb that picture. But, I will."

He pulled her close and started slow dancing, pulling her as close to him as possible. He found the zipper in the back and slowly worked it down as they continued dancing. She stepped out of her shoes and kicked them away as he untied and disposed of his. The zipper hit bottom and Paul's hands started caressing Ellen's lower back. Then, he worked his way up, feeling her warm skin, smelling the light perfume she was wearing.

She started humming along to one of their favorite Hawaiian songs, and he joined in as he pulled the dress forward. Ellen danced just the right way and soon the dress was history. Paul stepped back and observed that Ellen had on a revealing Hawaiian bikini.

He pulled her close again as their lips met. He just couldn't get enough. His lips trailed down to her neck and around to her ear. She giggled and pulled him close. He reached around to untie her top, hesitating just a second in case she wanted to object. Instead she kissed him harder and helped. It was gone. She pulled his shirt out of his pants and tugged it off him. They mashed together, he finally broke the kiss, took her hand and headed for the bedroom.

Around 1:00 in the morning Paul stirred. He didn't remember going to sleep, just holding Ellen in his arms. It was so great. She stirred, sat up and said, "Did we ever put out the candles? And, we never did eat dinner. Are you hungry?"

"Yes, I sure am, but not for food." He threw himself on top of her and started kissing her. She returned the favor and soon the sheets were twisted every which way.

They agreed to have breakfast downstairs at the famous Embassy Suites, and soon were heading back to Ellen's apartment. "I've got all week off, but I bet *you* were supposed to be to work, weren't you?"

"Yes, but I called in and made up a story about a morning meeting. I'm good.

We going to tell anybody?"

"Not unless we get cornered. I'm not ashamed, so it's no big problem for me.

You?"

"Not a problem. Except I want to do this every night, so it might be a bit obvious."

"Me too, but it won't happen. There is too much going on now. We'll make time for us. It feels so good to be free to love you with all my heart. Stop over tomorrow night. I know you're busy tonight." She leaned to him so they could kiss goodbye. Paul pulled away from Ellen's apartment feeling great. No...*better than great!*

Two days later, Steve reminisced as the three-of-them finished dinner. "You know guys, I didn't mention this before, but in the hospital I got real attached to my nurse." Holding his hand up, he continued. "I know, I know. This is common. Some kind of obligation factor. But, after being gone from there, I don't miss the hospital, but I miss her. Sara. Sara Forsyth. And, you know," he said as he settled back in the easy chair, stroked his chin and looked at the ceiling, "I think she liked me."

Ellen put her wine glass down and was about to speak, but Steve continued.

"Oh it could be that she felt sorry for me and was trying to keep my spirits up, but I think it was more than that. I mean, at first she was patronizing, but for the last several months it hasn't been that way." Sitting back up and gaining eye contact with Paul and Ellen he said, "And, since my most favorite girl is my sister, and, besides, she has a number one man, I just might find nurse Sara and have a serious talk with her. I do have to get her car back before she calls the cops." He leaned back in the chair, spread his legs out, put both hands behind his head and asked, "Speaking of serious, what about you two?"

"Well, ah, we ah," sputtered Paul.

"We're good friends," said Ellen, looking at Paul and taking his hand. "No, we're more than good friends. I think our future is taking shape for us now." She looked alternately at Paul and Steve.

"Yes, Ellen and I have had quite the experiences. You know some of it. We've been to the top. We've been to the bottom, you might say, and back towards the top again. From this vantage point now, it's a lot easier to make plans. We're in no rush, Steve. We're both mature adults. We've got the time to let things unfold. Hey," said Paul, "I'm taking tomorrow off. What say we head for Lake of the Isles and hike around there and Calhoun?"

"Good idea," replied Steve, "only, the Air Force is sending a man up here tomorrow to interview me and prepare for my discharge. Let's see. That's at 10:00 and shouldn't take more than an hour or so. Why don't you come over for breakfast? Missy can prepare a feast for us around 9:00." He turned and winked at her. "Then you both can sit in on the big Air Force review. How about it?" They all agreed, and Paul left to get a few things done before his day off.

Sara Forsyth sat up wearily on the edge of her bed. *Four days of the flu bug is enough for anybody*, she thought. She wobbled toward the Holiday Inn bathroom for the hundredth time. Her robe brushed the room service tray and tipped a half a cup of cold chicken noodle soup onto the rug. "Damn," she muttered, fetching the big white bath towel to soak up the remains. "Well, at least I got *something* done right today," she said out loud. She took another look at the address and phone number of Ellen Nantucket. She looked at the phone but decided, again, to go there in person. She was sure Steve was staying there. Tomorrow she would be strong enough. The thought caused her to shiver. Or, was it the flu?

Back at Ellen's apartment, breakfast went over big, and the three companions were in rare form for early morning. The day was indeed beautiful, and the anticipation of spending it together, hiking through old memories while making new ones, spiked the atmosphere.

Ellen heard the door buzzer, checked her watch, and announced, "The US Air Force has arrived."

Sara noticed how sweaty her palms were. The steering wheel of the rental car was slippery in her hands as she drove into a Standard station. She was in the right area, she knew, but she was still lost. The attendant pointed the way and told her she had a short, five-minute drive. Now, butterflies were bouncing off the walls of her stomach like a hail storm. She didn't notice the car pull up beside her as she was pulling away from the pumps. The driver honked loudly, just about causing Sara to lose control. She managed to jam on the brakes, gave the man a *'sorry, I'll be more careful'* look, and pulled slowly away.

Sergeant Dunnigan laid out several sheets from his briefcase that explained the benefits due Steve – some from his POW days and some for his disability. Dunnigan was very personable and well-suited for this job.

Sara had parked her car in front of the apartment, and was referring for the twentieth time to the now wrinkled paper that had Ellen's address and apartment number. She opened the car door, stood up, smoothed her tan blazer, and headed for the apartment building.

"Looks like your files are pretty complete," said Steve, "How much have you got on me?"

"Quite a bit," replied Dunnigan, as he rummaged through his briefcase. "You know the Air Force did a heck of a lot of research on you when they found out who you *weren't*."

There was a light knock on the apartment door. "Did someone knock?" Ellen asked.

"I think so," said Steve, absently.

"Okay, I'll get it." Ellen walked to the door.

"Oh, yes. Here it is," said Dunnigan, holding up a sheet of onionskin. "We go all the way back to where you were two months old, Steve, and you'd just been adopted by the Nantuckets," he glanced over to the door where a young lady was standing, "who then had a girl of their own, name of Ellen, about a year later."

EPILOGUE
MAY 1975

"Now that we've all had a more normal week, or at least sort of normal, can we talk about a few things?" Ellen was determined to get some answers and share her feelings. They had all gotten together several times just to get more acquainted, or reacquainted, as the case may be, but had not discussed anything very meaningful. Now they were sitting on Ellen's deck after a nice steak fry. "And, I have some news."

"Ellen, what's the news?"

"In just a bit. For now, I just want to talk about us. I mean, here we sit, together, Sara, Paul," she put her arm around his shoulder and gave it a squeeze, "my fabulous long lost brother," she paused to regain her composure, "and me. Two weeks ago, I thought Steve had long been dead, Paul was walking out of my life forever, and I didn't even know *you,* wonderful, beautiful Sara." She motioned, palm up towards Sara. "You're the sister I never had. Wow! What a ride! And, hang on, I'll get to my news in a minute. After our parents died, even though I was sixteen and knew better, I dreamt of marrying my brother. I know it's weird, but looking back, he was my only rock, and without him I was lost. Steve," she paused and looked at just him for a moment, "you were always so good to me...so good to me. That's why I could never completely love another. And, when I heard you were adopted, the fleeting thought flew through my mind that we possibly could get married and my teenage dream could come true. But, uh no. That really would be way too weird!" They all laughed. "But, now I feel a new sense of freedom to love another with all my heart." She put her hand on her chest and looked over at Paul.

214

"Paul, could I?" she said, raising her eyebrows. Paul gave a slight nod and a big smile. She continued, "There's good news and bad news. The bad news is Paul and I are *not* engaged. But, the good news is we've talked about it, and we will be *getting* engaged!" Sara and Steve stood and gave generous hugs all around, along with loud congratulations. "More good news…Paul is going to go into my kitchen and bring out four glasses and some fancy champagne we bought yesterday, aren't you, Paul?"

"What? Oh—yes, I'll get right on it."

Glasses were filled, and emptied amidst light conversation. Soon, Ellen stood up and announced, "Time for dessert! I'm going to get it ready."

"I'll help," offered Sara, and followed her into the kitchen.

"And, I've got to see a man about a horse," said Steve, struggling a bit as he tried to get up.

Now alone at the table, Paul leaned for the champagne bottle and filled his glass, then settled back into his chair. He knew this night almost didn't happen and still felt a bit awkward. A couple nights after Steve's miraculous reappearance, Paul had requested time together – just the three of them. Wanting to come clean, he explained in detail the plan he and Chris had put together, taking heavy blame for Chris' demise and the damage Chris had done. He even brought up the bank construction flaws, although reassured them that nothing would ever come of it. There was no desire left in him to carry out any of those plans. None of the banks had been accessed, nor would they ever be.

"I just want both of you to know the whole truth. You can turn me in to the authorities, ask me to get out of your lives forever…whatever you think I should do, I'll do it. Ellen, you mean more to me than anybody in my life and I want you to think of yourself in this decision. I take full responsibility. Whatever happens is because of what I did."

Ellen and Steve sat in silence for many seconds, looking at each other, looking at Paul, both clearly at a loss for words.

"If you want me to go so you can talk with each other, I'll be glad to go," said Paul, as he hung his head and sighed deeply.

Finally, Ellen said, "I don't know all the legal angles, but so far I don't see that you did anything wrong. You might have in the future, but you didn't yet. I feel so bad about Chris. This past year, I tried to avoid him because I could sense he had deep troubles. There's a piece of me that feels guilty, feeling like I should have done more. Paul," she said with an understanding tone, "you didn't encourage him to become violent. He was an adult making his own decisions. Like so many back from the war, he was damaged goods and did not get the help he needed."

"For once, I agree with my sister. There are thousands of unfortunate side effects of this or any war. Chris was one of them, along with his victims. Not your fault."

"Yes," said Ellen, adding to Steve's sentiments, Paul, I know you have a gentle soul. I love you. I want to be with you. We make a great couple. You have to realize it is not your fault. You have to forgive yourself so we can move on. I've carried enough baggage for a whole wagon train full of people. I'm an expert at that, and I'm coming around, and so can you."

"Some chocolate mousse?" Paul was startled back to reality by Sara serving dessert and half-dropping the lemonade pitcher on the glass table.

"Oh—sorry, did I wake you?" she laughed.

"No, just thinking."

"By the way," Steve said as he settled back down, "Missy, tell us your news. The engagement or pre-engagement, or whatever bill of goods Romeo here sold you, wasn't the actual news." He gave Paul a wry smile. "I already know, but tell Paul and Sara. It's exciting."

"Well, you know that Mrs. Thoms had a spell a little while ago and was in the hospital, right? You know her sister was in business with her until about twenty years ago, then moved to New York and had her own similar business there. Maybe you *didn't* know that part. But anyway, when I was in Japan and China, both times her sister took time off from her New York store to come to Minneapolis to fill in for me, because she has an excellent manager in New York who can run things just fine. So, between wanting to spend more time with her sister and her health scare, Mrs. Thoms has decided she wants to retire. Guess what?" Ellen said, lightly clapping her hands together, giddy. "We had a long talk this week and she wants *me* to buy the business. I've been like the daughter she never had. For her it's not about the money – she's had plenty of it, and after her husband died ten years ago, she had even more. She said she was mainly concerned that the business would successfully continue on into the future. She said I am the only one she trusts. Can you believe it?"

"I had an accountant I trust sit in with us. After a couple of his suggestions, we finalized the deal and signed papers. Afterward, he assured me it was a very *sweet* deal for me. He emphasized the word sweet about three times. I thought so, too. And, if that weren't amazing enough, Steve is going to take courses for a business degree and work with me at the same time."

"My gosh," Sara said, "what does Steve know about the fashion business? For most of the time I've known him, he's been in a hospital gown! He's never even said the word *dress*, or *fashion*, or anything like that." She laughed.

"You'd be surprised. Since he's been staying with me, we've talked about this and even had our own little brainstorming session."

"What did you come up with?" interjected Paul. "Shorter skirts?" He looked at Steve and laughed.

"No, Ellen replied, "actually some good ideas. I hate to admit it, but our clientele does not want to buy dresses at just any store, nor do they want to be in a shop where *ordinary* women might shop. It's just a fact of business. Our small store in one of the elite malls is going to take over a larger space that just became available. We were figuring on giving up our lease on the smaller space, but Steve had a brilliant idea. Get this – he thinks we could keep both and use the smaller store to serve clients *by appointment only*. Now that's exclusive! Definitely something our clientele would like. Also, besides dresses, it's time to offer more pant suits and even designer jeans. Our customers are…how should I say it, not super thin, on average, so we need to offer nicely designed, larger sizes. Some of our better customers have a harder time getting around as they get older, so another far out idea he had was a limo service: we pick them up, bring them to the store, they shop, and we take them home again. And, get this! What about an Annual Tea and Fashion Show for *invitation-only* clients. An event like that could draw hundreds and create some excitement. One of our New York suppliers is toying with going on the road to various cities for a three-day designer-dress tour. They bring the latest styles straight from Paris to our flagship store for 'three days only.' Ideas? Oh yes, Steve has ideas!"

"Wow, can we buy stock in this enterprise?" asked Paul. "Sounds excellent! By the way, Steve, not to be nosy, but being nosy, what are you and Sara's plans?"

Sara answered, "I got my own apartment this week. I also called my former boss, and, uh, boyfriend, if you can call a 50-year-old a boy, and actually we had a pleasant talk. He admitted he was married to his work and never did get over the loss of his wife—ah, to cancer. And, the age difference was too great. He suspected I wouldn't be around long. Knowing I'd need a job, he contacted a doctor who has the same position at the Minneapolis VA. That was thoughtful, and he even put in a good word for me. Turns out they have an opening similar to what I was doing. I'm going for an interview this coming week. The doctor assures me the job is mine, if all is as it seems."

"You *know* what I'm going to be doing," Steve said, "going to class and working for Ms. Dress Tyrant. Pray for me," he laughed. "No, ah, Sara and I are kinda new to each other outside the hospital, so we'll date awhile, then see what happens. I will say this, I really, really, really like this lady!" he said, as he patted her shoulder. "Next week, I'm going apartment hunting. Living with my sister cramps my style. But, I'll be looking for a place between here and the U.

"Well, alright!" Paul said. "Everybody get some champagne. Here's a toast. To us – God bless us all!" Their glasses and eyes met in unified celebration.

Saturday morning rolled around, and it was shaping up to be a beautiful day. As usual, Paul took the newspaper and a cup of coffee out to his sunlit terrace. Placing the mug on the table, he sat down on the rustic patio chair, ready to catch up with today's news. He unfolded the paper, and on the front page right below the fold, a headline caught

219

his eye: "Senator Ruskins from Ohio Dies in Mysterious Car Accident." The smaller headline read: "Witnesses report hearing a rifle shot at the exact same time." The story went on to explain that the car appeared to have blown a passenger-side tire while traveling next to a large ravine on the right. The car had plunged down, rolled many times, and killed all three occupants.

The End

AFTERTHOUGHTS

Vietnam Vengeance is just a novel, and maybe that's all there is to it. This novel's purpose is to raise awareness of the awful fallout from war; any war. What is depicted in these pages is mostly mild compared to real life, except for Chris' vengeful actions. Some wars seem to be necessary. In my opinion, we had to participate in the two world wars, no matter the consequences to individuals. But as for other wars, I'm not so sure.

What did we accomplish in Korea or Vietnam that was worth the body count, injuries, and the trauma inflicted on our soldiers, their families and loved ones?

The fictional story shows several perspectives; perspectives of participants and non-participants. It's the ripple effect: throw a stone into a quiet pond and the ripples continue their outward journey, affecting the calm for quite a distance. In our story, Paul became someone he would not normally be. Chris did as well, although in a different direction: taking many lives. He carried the battlefield with him, with all the destruction that ensued. Ellen could not have a normal relationship with a man due to her war trauma. Steve is permanently handicapped. And, on it goes.

Our decision-makers probably sit in their war room, estimate a body count, and then try to make a good decision. But, they do not look deep enough. Every casualty and injury has a tremendous impact on many lives for a lifetime. Think of the wives who lost their husbands, or the husbands who lost their wives, the children who grow up without a parent, the thousands of potential children never born, and the anniversaries never celebrated. Lives are ripped apart – some literally, some emotionally. Some recover from their emotional and physical wounds and move on in life. Some do not. Even now, decades later, it is hard to go two days without reading of some consequence of the Vietnam War. Almost every day something bad happens as a result of our presence in the Middle East. Just recently, the paper reported about a mother taking her own life because her son had been killed in the Middle East conflict. After four years of grieving, she could not stand it anymore and wanted to be with him. Watch the papers. The war ripples move nearly every day.

Injured soldiers live, but with the horrors of war, as do their families. It is a difficult adjustment back to civilian life, so there is a higher rate of divorce, unemployment and mental instability. This brings much stress to children, spouses, parents, siblings, and extended family.

Is what we are doing in these *conflicts*, and the devastating consequences, worth being foisted on even one American family? Multiply that by 58,000+ killed in action and the 153,000+ wounded in Vietnam. In Korea, more than 33,000 were killed in action and over 103,000 wounded.

Looking back, even if we accomplished something in these *wars*, was it worth anywhere near the terrible cost?

©2015 Keith Kluis

ACKNOWLEDGMENTS

To my end table drawers, which held my unfinished novel for 30+ years, keeping it safe.

To my wife, Ruth, who encouraged me to finish that novel and get it out of the drawer. And then, encouraged me even more.

To my best high school buddy, Dr. Paul Nelson, Professor Emeriti at NDSU, who, when I instructed him to read this things to see if there was any hope—but not to edit it—couldn't help himself and gave me many pointers.

To my son, Kevin, who was the first to read it and also helped with editing. To Kris and Kat who took time to read and comment.

To Stephanie Hall, Head Librarian at the Meinders Community Library in Pipestone, Minnesota, who took time from her busy home and professional schedule to critically read the story and offer many good suggestions.

To Judy who edited a chapter, then edited a bit more to get me on the right track.

To Dr. Bill, Donn and others (you know who you are) who read the many drafts of the manuscript and gave me encouraging feedback.

And finally, to my publishers, Krista Dunk and Deborah McLain, for their editing, suggestions and making this project come to life. You're the best!

AUTHOR BIO:

Author Keith Kluis' career included traveling the United States as a seminar leader associated with residential housing. While serving in the US Army Reserves in the 1960's, Keith saw no action, but his stint in the military and living through the Vietnam War era inspired him to write this novel. *Vietnam Vengeance: One Divided by Two* is his first work of war-related fiction.

Now retired, Keith enjoys his grandchildren, Tanner, Makenna and Kaedin, playing tennis, walking, traveling, and reading. He and his wife live in both Minnesota and Arizona, splitting their time between the two.

www.keithkluis.com
keithkluis@gmail.com

Vietnam Vengeance is proudly published by:

Creative Force Press

www.CreativeForcePress.com

Do You Have a Book in You?

www.ingramcontent.com/pod-product-compliance
Lightning Source LLC
Chambersburg PA
CBHW071153260626
47162CB00003B/1025